DEATH IN KENSINGTON

An Augusta Peel Mystery Book 8

EMILY ORGAN

The Augusta Peel Series

Chapter 1

'YOU'RE NOT SMILING, LOLA.'

'We're not supposed to.'

'That was for the previous photograph. I want you smiling for this one. Didn't you hear me explain it? All the other girls did.'

Lola glared at the other girls.

They were all wearing woollen fur-trimmed dresses in sapphire blue, emerald green, and magenta pink.

Lola forced a smile and Cedric Langley took the photograph.

'I'm too hot,' she said, peeling off her thick gloves. 'Why are we wearing these clothes when it's eighty degrees outside?'

'It's the autumn and winter collection,' said Sylvia. 'Isn't it obvious?'

'Can you put your gloves back on please, Lola,' said Cedric.

'No, I'm too hot. Can't I just put my hands in my pockets?'

'No, we need to see the gloves.'

'Why?'

'Because they're part of the collection.'

'Well, they're inside out now. It's going to take me ages to turn them the right way out.'

Cedric marched over to her. 'Give them here, then.' He snatched the gloves from her and turned them the right way out. 'Here.' He thrust them back at her.

Lola sulked as she put them back on.

'Can you stop messing about now, Lola?' said Daphne. 'We all want to get on. We've got three more outfits to go yet.'

'Three?'

'Yes, three,' said Cedric, striding back to his camera. 'Now come on. Let's get some good pictures.'

Lola cooperated for a while, and Cedric's mood improved. She was difficult, but she was easily the most beautiful of Miss Kingsley's models. Every outfit looked perfect on her. She was tall, slender, and long-limbed. Her face had sharp, defined cheekbones, full lips and eyes like two dark pools. The camera adored her.

His good mood didn't last for long.

'I'm tired,' said Lola. 'Can we have a break?'

Cedric clenched his teeth. 'You can have five minutes.'

'Five? I want ten.'

'Alright then. Ten. And not a minute over.'

Lola was infuriating. She tested the patience of everyone around her. The girl had to be careful in this industry. If she upset the wrong person, who knew what might happen?

Chapter 2

'YOU'VE DONE a remarkable job repairing this, Augusta.' Fred examined the copy of *Bleak House* by Charles Dickens. Bound in red Morocco leather with gilt lettering on the spine, it was a heavy book with almost a thousand pages.

'I enjoyed working on it,' said Augusta.

They stood at the counter in her bookshop. Sparky the canary eyed Augusta from his cage, waiting expectantly for some more birdseed to be passed to him through the bars.

'We need to decide on a price for the book,' said Fred.

'A shilling and sixpence.'

'Really? I think two shillings and sixpence would be better.'

'Would anyone spend that much on it?'

'Of course they would, Augusta! It's a lovely book which is in excellent condition now you've repaired it.'

'Well, we could try two shillings and sixpence,' said Augusta. 'And after it sits unsold on the shelf for a month, we can reduce the price.'

Fred laughed. 'Alright then. But I'm sure someone will buy it for two and six.'

The bell above the shop door rang as a young woman stepped inside. She wore a pale blue summer dress and round spectacles. She had an attractive heart-shaped face and bobbed hair.

'Can we help you with anything?' asked Augusta.

'Have you got anything by Charles Dickens?' she asked.

'Yes, we have.' Augusta smiled and pointed at the book in Fred's hand.

'This is *Bleak House*,' Fred said to the customer. 'Do you have a particular book in mind?'

The shrill ring of the telephone behind the counter interrupted them. Augusta answered it while Fred continued dealing with the customer.

'Hello Augusta, it's Philip.'

'Where are you? I thought you were in your office upstairs.'

He chuckled. 'I am.'

'Why are you telephoning me?'

'I thought it would be fun.'

'Rather than walk down a staircase?'

'Yes. It's rather lazy of me, isn't it?'

'What are you telephoning about? I feel like I'm being summoned by the master of the household.'

'I've got someone here with me at the moment. He's asking for my help with something, and we think you could help us too. Do you have a spare five minutes?'

Augusta glanced at Fred and the young woman. They were chatting happily. 'Alright then. Who's with you?'

'Come up and see.'

Augusta wondered if Philip had a surprise in store for her as she climbed the stairs to his detective agency. But the man who was sitting with Philip in his office was fairly unremarkable. He was a stout grey-haired gentleman whom she recognised as a detective from Scotland Yard.

The two men got to their feet. 'Do you remember Detective Inspector Morris, Augusta?' said Philip.

'Yes, I do.' She shook the detective's hand.

'It's a pleasure to meet you again, Mrs Peel.' They had last met when Philip had taken a leave of absence from his work and Augusta had spoken to the detective when she had been worried about his whereabouts.

'I'm sorry about the telephone call, Augusta,' said Philip as they sat down. 'I won't do it again. I thought it would be fun to try once.'

'And was it fun?'

'I suppose it was. A little.'

Augusta turned to Detective Inspector Morris. 'You need our help?' she said.

'Yes,' he said. 'I need your detective skills.'

Chapter 3

'I've given Mr Fisher a brief explanation,' said Detective Inspector Morris. 'And he suggested you'd be able to help too, Mrs Peel. About three years ago, there was a burglary at the home of Lord and Lady Montpelier in Belgravia. A number of items were taken, including a rather valuable painting known as *Sunset at the Temple of Artemis.*'

'That sounds like a nice painting,' said Augusta, picturing a classical scene with a red-streaked sky.

'Perhaps I wasn't educated well enough,' said Philip. 'But what is the Temple of Artemis?' He addressed his question to the detective, who shrugged his shoulders. Both men then looked at Augusta.

'It's one of the seven wonders of the ancient world,' she said. 'It's an ancient Greek temple and its site was rediscovered at Ephesus about fifty years ago.'

'How do you know this?' asked Philip.

'Haven't you visited the display at the British Museum? Some of the fragments are displayed there.'

'No, I haven't. I must go and have a look,' said Philip.

'But let's concentrate on finding the painting first,' said

Detective Inspector Morris. 'I forget the name of the person who painted it, art isn't my strongest subject.' He pulled an envelope out of his pocket and took out a photograph. '"R. C. Riverhouse. 1798",' he read from the back of the photograph. 'That's who painted it. R. C. Riverhouse.'

He laid the photograph on Philip's desk, and they leant forward to examine it. The picture was sepia and a little blurry. It showed a ruined classical temple with fallen columns and a half-collapsed entablature. Three nymph-like women with flowing hair and diaphanous robes posed daintily by the structure while a dramatic sunset occupied the background.

Augusta squinted at the picture. 'I would like to see it in colour,' she said. 'I may be able to look up a better copy in a library. I'm sure it will have been catalogued in a book somewhere.'

'That's a good idea,' said the detective. 'I didn't think of that myself. Anyway, back to the details. The burglary at Lord and Lady Montpelier's home was very professional. The thieves knew what they were looking for and took only the most valuable items. They targeted a number of wealthy homes in Belgravia over a period of a few months. I'm happy to say the Flying Squad collared them.' He turned to Augusta. 'The Flying Squad is a new team of detectives which uses motor cars to patrol London and arrest thieves and other ne'er-do-wells. Thanks to their work, the Belgravia burglars are now serving long prison sentences.'

Augusta nodded politely. She had heard of the Flying Squad.

'There's a problem, though,' continued Detective Inspector Morris. 'We're having difficulty recovering some of the items stolen by the gang. These professional robbers sell on their spoils rather quickly. We've recovered some items, but many are still missing.'

'Including *Sunset at the Temple of Artemis?*'

'Absolutely, Mrs Peel. And although Lord Montpelier is grateful we imprisoned the gang, he's not particularly happy that we haven't been able to recover his favourite painting. And it's even more important that we find it because he is quite seriously ill.'

'Oh no,' said Philip. 'I didn't know that.'

'He's quite elderly and therefore weakened by age. He's informed me his doctor says he may not live to see the end of this year. So, as you can appreciate, he would like to see his painting again. We're fortunate he's funding us with a good sum of money to recover the painting, but we also find ourselves quite overworked at the present time. This is why I've come to you for help, Mr Fisher.'

'Very well. But this could be like looking for a needle in a haystack. Have you got any idea where the painting could be?'

'We've got an idea. There's an art dealer who goes by the name of Briggs. He's been placing advertisements in a fine art magazine recently. The Mayfair address he uses roused my suspicion because it's close to an address associated with a criminal art dealer who went by the name of Fleming. Now, I have a hunch that Briggs and Fleming are the same man. When things got too warm for Fleming, he laid low for a while before renaming himself as Briggs.'

'How do you know he has the painting?' asked Philip.

'I don't. But I know Fleming has worked with several criminal gangs in the past. He's well-presented and well-spoken and can easily fool unsuspecting buyers into purchasing stolen art. I suspect he's running out of money and has now invented himself as Briggs, so he can sell off a few things.'

'Can't you just go to the address and arrest him?' asked Augusta.

'We don't actually have any evidence yet that Briggs is trying to sell stolen art. I'm assuming he is, but we need evidence. We need someone to act as an interested buyer and hopefully see the painting in his possession. Once that's confirmed, then we can swoop in.'

'So this is an undercover job,' said Philip.

'Exactly. And he will be extremely wary about under-cover police officers posing as potential buyers. We have to tread very carefully indeed.'

'So this is why you'd like me to be involved,' said Augusta. 'Because I can't possibly be an undercover police officer?'

'Yes, correct, Mrs Peel! However,' he held up his hand in a warning gesture, 'Briggs is an unpleasant man. He's of the criminal class, and we don't want to leave you alone with a fellow like that. So you'll need to take someone with you.'

Augusta glanced at Philip.

'That's right, Augusta,' he said. 'Take me.'

'But surely he'll guess you're an undercover police officer?'

'I'm not a police officer anymore.'

'You know what criminals are like, Philip. They can spot a plainclothes detective, or even a former detective, at thirty yards.'

'Yes, this is a risk,' said Detective Inspector Morris. 'And it's a challenge I think we can overcome if the pair of you pose as a married couple.'

'Married?' Augusta felt herself blushing so much that she couldn't bring herself to look at Philip. 'I suppose it makes sense.'

'Yes I suppose it does,' said Philip. She wondered if he

felt happy about the proposal, but it was difficult to tell from his short response.

'So can I leave it with you?' said Detective Inspector Morris.

'Yes,' said Philip.

'I'll drop a file in tomorrow with all the details. As soon as you've come up with a plan, let me know.'

'We will do,' said Augusta.

'Wonderful.' The detective got to his feet and put on his hat. 'I'll speak to you again shortly, Mr and Mrs Fisher.'

Augusta felt herself blush again at the description as the detective left the room.

'It sounds like an interesting job, doesn't it, Augusta?' said Philip.

'Yes, it does. We did a lot of undercover work during the war, so hopefully it won't be too tricky.'

'No, I think we'll be fine. We'll make sure Lord Montpelier gets his precious painting back.' The telephone on Philip's desk rang. 'Oh, I'm sorry. I should answer this.'

Augusta excused herself and returned downstairs to the shop. To her surprise, Fred was still talking to the young woman. She was holding a heavy-looking shopping bag, and Augusta suspected Fred had sold her a few books.

They paused their conversation as Augusta reached the foot of the stairs.

'We were just discussing Miss Havisham in *Great Expectations*,' Fred said to her.

'Please don't stop on my account,' said Augusta, as she made her way to the shop counter.

'Oh, it's quite alright. I'd better get going,' said the young woman. 'I've just realised the time!'

'Yes, of course,' said Fred. 'And once you've finished those books, you know where to come for more.'

'Yes, I do.'

The pair smiled and held each other's gaze for a moment. Augusta busied herself with some papers behind the counter.

'Well, I'll be off,' said the young woman.

'It was lovely to meet you,' said Fred.

'And you.'

'Bye.'

Fred waited until the shop door had closed. 'Harriet bought your copy of *Bleak House*, Augusta.'

'For two and six?'

'Yes. We should have priced it at three shillings.'

'No, that would have been too much. Her name's Harriet, you say?'

Fred gave a coy smile. 'Yes. I told her my name, too. Just in case she comes back again.'

Augusta felt fairly sure she would.

Chapter 4

LADY HEREFORD CALLED in at Augusta's bookshop that afternoon. Her nurse wheeled her into the shop in her bath chair. The old lady wore a broad-brimmed summer hat trimmed with silk flowers.

'The weather's lovely today, Augusta. Have you been out in it yet?'

'Not yet.'

'I suppose you've been cooped up in this shop, haven't you? Never mind. We've just had a lovely stroll in Russell Square. Not that I stroll anymore, but you know what I mean.'

The nurse wheeled Lady Hereford to Sparky's cage on the counter.

'Have you been behaving yourself today?' she asked the canary.

'Yes, he has,' said Augusta. 'He's always on his best behaviour in the shop. But at home it can be a different matter.'

'Does he still avoid his cage at bedtime?'

'Yes, quite often.'

'You need to be stricter with him. Withhold his apple pieces if he doesn't comply.'

'I shall try that,' said Augusta, not intending to. 'I wasn't expecting you to visit today, Lady Hereford.' The old lady usually called on Augusta once or twice a week.

'I've come to invite you to something.'

'To what?' Augusta hoped it wasn't a party.

'A fashion show.'

'That's kind of you, Lady Hereford, but I'm not a very fashionable person.'

'Me neither. And I don't particularly want to go. But my niece's daughter, Daphne, is taking part, so I'm expected to. It's a show being put on in Kensington by Vivien Kingsley's fashion house. I take it you've heard of Kingsley?'

Augusta nodded. It was an expensive brand beyond her price range.

'To be honest with you, Augusta, my niece, Isabella, means well, but she's hard work. And so for her daughter, Daphne… well, she's a rather spoilt girl, I'm afraid. Prone to whining. I would really like some sensible company, so that's why I'm asking you.'

Augusta realised it would be difficult to refuse. 'Alright then. When is it?'

'Tomorrow afternoon. I realise it's short notice, but Isabella wasn't sure whether there'd be any spare tickets for friends and family. Unfortunately, it turned out that there were. It's at the Holland Park Rink. I'll collect you by taxi at two o'clock. Perhaps we'll even enjoy it. Who knows?'

Chapter 5

ONCE SHE HAD CLOSED her shop for the day, Augusta made some tea, then took it up to Philip in his office.

'Thank you, Augusta. How did you know I needed a cup of tea?'

'It was a lucky guess.' She sat herself in one of the easy chairs. 'We need to plan our visit to Mr Briggs.'

'Yes, we do.' Philip joined her in the other easy chair with his cup of tea in one hand and his notebook in the other. 'Scotland Yard is going to pay us quite handsomely for this work,' said Philip. 'Thanks to Lord Montpelier's donation.'

'The money will help your detective agency, Philip. But there's no need to pay me. I won't be able to give this much time, anyway. I have a shop to run.'

'I'll try not to take up too much of your time, Augusta. But I do insist on paying you.' He took a sip of tea. 'Now let's think about the characters we're going to play.'

'Characters?'

'Yes. This is undercover work. We need to take on characters.'

'I'm not an actor.'

'No, I realise that. But when you go undercover, you're pretending to be someone else. It's a form of acting, isn't it? Just as we did in Belgium during the war. But we're in peacetime now, so everything's a little safer. Now then, because I'm a former police officer and this Briggs chap is wary of people like me, I think you need to be the person who's most interested in the painting, Augusta. I can be your henpecked husband standing meekly behind you.'

'Henpecked?'

'Yes. I don't want to speak too much or deal with Briggs directly because he's going to be suspicious of me. If I can just be a meek husband who always agrees with his wife, then hopefully I'll come across as a dull character who he won't pay much attention to. On the other hand, Augusta, you'll need to be the loud, flamboyant type.'

'Loud and flamboyant, Philip? That's the opposite of what I am.'

Philip sighed. 'I realise that, Augusta. But you're playing a part. You can't just walk into his office as your-self. You're going to have to change your appearance and be someone completely different.'

'I know that. But do I have to be loud and flamboyant? Can't I choose how I can be?'

'Very well. But do you understand what I'm attempting to achieve here? You need to be the dominant one, the one who wants to buy the painting. I need to be the one who hangs back and nods and agrees with everything you say and do. But obviously, I do have a purpose, Augusta. Because if there's any trouble, I can protect you.'

'I think I need a bit of time to think about how I'm going to present myself.'

'Yes, by all means, have a think about it. And then you

can tell me tomorrow what sort of character you want to be.'

'Tomorrow?'

'Yes. We want to get on with this, don't we?'

'Yes. But I don't want to come up with something by tomorrow.'

Philip regarded her for a moment. 'Are you sure you want to do this?'

'Yes. But I don't like being hurried.'

'I'm sorry if you think I'm hurrying you. Are you feeling nervous about this?'

'I'm nervous about being married to you, that's for sure!'

They both laughed.

'Take all the time you need. And I shall think about my character.'

'Presumably if you're not going to say or do very much, then it won't take you long.'

'It will still take some time, Augusta. I need to ensure I can inhabit the character convincingly. I need to be very thorough about it. Even if I'm not saying or doing very much, my appearance and the manner in which I conduct myself needs to be carefully planned.'

Augusta thought Philip was in danger of taking the work too seriously. 'Surely all we need to do is turn up, pretend we're a married couple, then speak to Briggs about the works of art he's selling. And if he happens to show us *Sunset at the Temple of Artemis*, then we know he's got it, and we can tell the Yard.'

'That's the essence of it, yes. But it's important we stick to a plan. If Briggs realises we're working for Scotland Yard, then that could be the end of us, Augusta. This man could be ruthless.'

'I thought you said this was safer than the work we did in the war?'

'It is. But only a little bit.'

Chapter 6

THE FOLLOWING AFTERNOON, Augusta and Lady Hereford's taxi pulled up on Holland Park Road in Kensington. The driver helped Lady Hereford out of the motor car and Augusta helped her into the bath chair which had been strapped onto the back of the vehicle.

Holland Park Rink had been a popular roller-skating venue before the war. It had a grand, arched facade topped either side by two turrets. The building's name was emblazoned across the arch in bold brass lettering. Advertisements for future events, including dog shows and boxing matches, were attached to the railings.

A steady stream of people was passing through the ornate iron gates. Augusta followed them, pushing Lady Hereford in her bath chair. A steward at the entrance checked their tickets and ushered them through.

Inside, the cavernous room echoed with music and lively chatter. It was decorated with elaborate floral displays, and a string quartet played a waltz. A temporary stage had been erected at one end of the room. A raised walkway led out from it and was surrounded on three sides by rows of chairs. These were almost filled with ladies in fancy hats and a few gentlemen. The rink-side seats were full, as was the gallery seating from where spectators could look down on the stage and walkway.

'I don't know where you're going to put me, Augusta,' shouted Lady Hereford over the noise. 'It looks rather full.'

Another steward spotted them and guided them to a place close to the stage, where he moved two chairs out of the way to make space for the bath chair.

'Now you have one of the best seats in the house,' he said with a grin. Lady Hereford thanked him, and Augusta sat on a chair next to her.

'Auntie! I'm so glad you came!'

A middle-aged lady in a plum purple crepe dress practically fell onto Lady Hereford and embraced her.

'Hello Isabella,' said the old lady.

'I'm so proud of Daphne today!' She stood upright again and adjusted her plum purple hat.

'I'm sure you are. She's done very well for herself.'

'Do you know it's possible these days for a young woman to make a career out of modelling clothes?'

'A career? Goodness. I'm sure Daphne is marvellous at it.'

'The pay isn't very good. Miss Kingsley only pays five pounds a week.'

'Is that all? It's lucky Daphne comes from a wealthy family then. This is my good friend Augusta Peel. You remember Mrs Peel, don't you?'

Isabella gave Augusta a blank look. 'No, I don't think we've met.'

Augusta recalled meeting Isabella at a dinner at Lady Hereford's home when she had first arrived in London. Isabella now looked her up and down, possibly wondering why someone in a dowdy blouse and skirt would be interested in a fashion show.

'I'm looking forward to seeing Daphne's outfits,' said Lady Hereford.

'So am I! She's going to look quite beautiful, I'm sure of it. Oh look, can you see Vivien Kingsley?' She pointed across the walkway at a lady with silver bobbed hair who was wearing a black velvet jacket and pleated skirt. The jacket was trimmed with bright pink ribbon and buttons and a line of pink buttons ran down one side of the skirt. The designer was talking to a lady in orange who had a cascade of beaded necklaces around her neck. Standing close by was a tall, pale-faced man with a square jaw. 'That's the Russian duke with her. Nikolai Volkov.'

'London is practically overrun with exiled Russian dukes these days,' said Lady Hereford. 'He's courting Miss Kingsley is he?'

Isabella nodded.

'They make an interesting pairing,' said Lady Hereford.

'But they're quite devoted to one another I've heard,' said her niece. 'I'd better get back to my seat. Let's find each other again after the show.'

She went on her way and Augusta watched the Russian duke for a moment. He looked a little bored.

'How funny that Daphne could make a career out of this,' said Lady Hereford to Augusta. 'She was always an odd-looking child. Quite angular in the face and no shape to her at all. She's tall and slender. A little too slender, I'd say. But I suppose that's the fashion these days, isn't it?'

A po-faced gentleman with a camera positioned himself alongside them and glanced around. He had oiled hair and was impeccably attired in a burgundy jacket with thin stripes of gold. He wore burgundy trousers, a gold waistcoat, a lace cravat and a large white carnation as a buttonhole.

Augusta watched him from the corner of her eye as he sucked in his cheeks and surveyed the scene.

Then he spoke to them. 'I'm terribly sorry,' he said to Lady Hereford, 'but you're going to have to move.'

The old lady allowed a long, uncomfortable pause to pass. 'I beg your pardon?' she said eventually.

'You have to move. I'm Cedric Langley, the photographer and I need to stand here to take photographs.'

'Aren't there any other places where you can take photographs?'

'Yes. But I need to move around during the show, you see. I'm currently identifying the best vantage points. And you're sitting in one of them.'

'This is the only space which can accommodate my bath chair,' said Lady Hereford. 'So I'm not inclined to move, I'm afraid. There's simply nowhere else to put me.'

Mr Langley pulled at his cravat. 'It's the fault of the organisers,' he said. 'They haven't thought about the layout of this place properly. But I have to work with what I've been given, and that means asking a few people to move, I'm afraid. You're not the only one. I'm going to be asking those ladies over there to move, too.'

'You certainly know how to make yourself popular, don't you?' said Lady Hereford.

He gave a sniff. 'This is a prestigious event. The photographs from this show will be featured in all the society magazines. I'm afraid I really don't have time to negotiate with everyone. Instead, I require some understanding that I have an important job to do.'

'And I've got an important job to do, too. I'm going to be watching my great niece in this show. It's been difficult enough trying to secure a place where I can see the show properly. I simply don't want to miss her.'

He raised an eyebrow. 'Your great-niece is in the show?'

'Yes, that's right. Daphne Chatsworth.'

'Miss Chatsworth? I see.'

'You know her?'

'Yes. I photograph Miss Chatsworth quite regularly for Kingsley. If you're her great aunt, then are you Lady Hereford, by any chance?'

'Yes.'

'She's mentioned you a few times.'

'How nice of her. Do you still want me to move?'

'No!' He held out a palm to stop her. 'There's no need for you to move at all, Lady Hereford. Please accept my apologies for speaking to you in the way I did just now. I get nervous before a show and my manner can be quite brusque at times. I'm so terribly sorry. I hope you'll accept my apology.'

'While I can understand you being nervous, Mr Langley, you should remember your manners before you speak to people.'

'If I had known you were Lady Hereford—'

'It doesn't matter who I am, does it? A little politeness goes a long way, you know.'

'It does.' He gave her a little bow. 'I shall go and look for other vantage points.'

'What an obnoxious man,' said Lady Hereford once the photographer had left. 'I wonder if everybody in the fashion industry is as unpleasant as that? It wouldn't surprise me. It's probably similar to show business. A world with an awful lot of people thinking they're much more important than they are.'

'His mood soon changed when he realised you were important though, didn't it?'

'I'm not that important though, am I Augusta? I have a title which sounds impressive and people kowtow to me. Just think what you could do with your title, Augusta. You could revert to the name Lady Rebecca Buchanan and prance around this place in an expensive dress. Everyone would fall at your feet.'

Augusta laughed. 'And I would hate it. I'm a lot happier being Augusta Peel than Lady Rebecca.'

'Good for you, Augusta. I admire you for choosing your path.' The quartet stopped playing, and the lights dimmed. Then the quartet struck up a new tune. 'Here we go,' said Lady Hereford. 'It's time for the show!'

Chapter 7

A PROCESSION of young women paraded onto the stage. They wore knee-length silk dresses in shades of gold, emerald, red, silver, and pink. Each dress was embellished with a long silken scarf in a matching colour. The scarves draped from shoulders and waistlines. They looped around necks and hung in long bows at necklines.

The models held their poses on the stage for a moment, before proceeding along the walkway so everyone could get a good view of their outfits. Each woman maintained an impassive expression with a steady gaze which avoided all eye contact with the audience.

Lady Hereford pointed out Daphne to Augusta. She was tall and elegant, like her companions, and had prominent cheekbones and a sharp nose. Her dress was a glimmering gold and had full sleeves which ballooned at the wrist.

Augusta spotted Cedric Langley, the photographer, lurking by the walkway and taking photographs. Daphne and her companions filed off the stage as the music changed and a second group made a well-coordinated arrival. They wore travelling coats in turquoise, burgundy, magenta, and olive green with matching hats and handbags. Some coats were trimmed with fur at the collar and hem while others had wide plaid collars and large cuffs. The hats were brimless and fitted close to the head, with some appearing to be little more than a wrap of thick fabric.

'I don't like some of these styles,' said Lady Hereford. 'Whatever happened to a proper hat?'

She was even less impressed with the parade of tea gowns which came next. Augusta had heard they were the latest fashion to come from Paris. They were light garments in shades of lilac, lemon, and dusky pink with lace panelling in the bodices and skirts. Silk flowers were sewn onto necklines and waistlines.

'They may as well be parading about in their petticoats,' muttered Lady Hereford.

The continuous colourful processions meant there was always something new to look at. Augusta realised she was enjoying herself. The evening gowns made her wish she had a special event to dress up for as she admired the elegant ankle-length dresses. They draped from the shoulder or waist in folds of silk, and some featured bold geometric prints. Others were influenced by the Orient, with intricate embroidery, beads and tassels.

Lady Hereford's great niece, Daphne, conducted herself perfectly. Augusta imagined the frantic activity in the changing rooms as the women hurriedly changed in and out of their outfits. There was no hint of any backstage chaos as they calmly showed off the clothes in front of the audience.

As the show concluded, all the models gathered together on the stage. There looked to be about thirty of them. Vivien Kingsley strode out from among them to receive a standing ovation from the audience. The designer grinned and bowed as she received the applause. The show had concluded, and everyone appeared to have enjoyed themselves.

The models began to file off the stage, the lights went up, and the audience readied itself to leave.

'What did you think, Augusta?' asked Lady Hereford.

'I enjoyed it more than I thought I would. I'm even thinking about buying a new handbag now.'

Lady Hereford laughed. 'Don't get carried away with it, Augusta. Now then, let's try to get out of here reasonably quickly so I don't have to speak to Isabella again. I've shown my face and that's all that matters.'

Augusta got up to manoeuvre Lady Hereford's bath chair when a flash of movement caught her eye. Daphne was running out onto the stage in stockinged feet. She'd lifted the hem of her silver evening gown so she wouldn't trip on it. She gripped it in both hands as she called out to the audience. Her face was shocked and pale.

'Is there a doctor here?' she cried out. 'We need a doctor! Quickly!'

Chapter 8

TRAMLINES of dark makeup ran down Daphne's face as she was comforted by her mother outside the changing rooms. She struggled to get her words out between gasping sobs.

'I was the first one to get back to the changing rooms,' she said. 'I thought I was the only one in there at first and then I saw Lola there, just lying on the floor. I thought she'd fainted. But when I got closer… Oh, it was awful! The scarf was so tight around her neck…'

'Oh dear,' said Lady Hereford. 'That's dreadful.'

'It was obvious she was dead. Someone must have strangled her with the scarf she was wearing. She couldn't have done something like that herself.'

'Take one of these, Daphne,' said her mother, holding out a bottle of pills beneath her nose. 'It will make you feel better.'

'What are they?'

'Just something which will help you feel better. Go on, take one.' Isabella tipped a little white tablet into her palm and held it up to Daphne's mouth. 'Just take it. Go on.'

Her daughter kept her mouth closed.

'I don't think Daphne wants to take it,' said Lady Hereford. 'Tablets won't make her feel better after what she's just witnessed. It's an absolute tragedy. She needs a bit of time to calm herself and cope with the enormity of what's happened.'

'Which is why she needs something to help calm her down.'

'It won't help. She'll need her wits about her for when the police arrive.'

'The police?' said Isabella. 'What would they want with her?'

'Daphne was the first to find Lola on the floor,' said Lady Hereford. 'The police will want to take a statement from her. But there's nothing to worry about, they'll be perfectly pleasant about it, I'm sure. Augusta can tell you more about what they do. A close friend of hers used to be a detective inspector at Scotland Yard.'

'I don't want the police talking to Daphne.'

'I'm afraid you don't have any choice in the matter, my dear. They'll speak to as many people as possible. So the best thing you can do is comfort Daphne and reassure her she'll be alright. At least she's still with us. Unlike her poor friend Lola.'

Daphne burst into tears again.

'Oh Daphne, that's enough,' said her mother. She was clearly struggling to cope with her daughter's emotions. Augusta stepped away for a few moments to get her thoughts in order.

They were standing in a corridor between the rink-side seating and the ladies' changing rooms. Augusta recalled the final section of the show when all the models had appeared on the stage with Vivien Kingsley. For some reason, Lola hadn't been on the stage with them. And someone had used that opportunity to strangle her with her scarf.

But who? And why?

Augusta estimated there had been two or three hundred people at the show. She tried to recall if she had noticed anyone looking out of place or acting suspiciously. But no one came to mind.

The clue to finding the person who attacked Lola was connected to Lola herself. Augusta felt sure the model must have known her attacker. She couldn't imagine a complete stranger entering the changing rooms and murdering whoever they found there.

Daphne would be able to tell Augusta more about Lola, but the girl would have to endure questions from the police first. She was understandably upset, and Augusta couldn't imagine her coping well with the interview. Although Lady Hereford had sought to reassure Isabella, Augusta knew the person who discovered a body could be considered a suspect until proven otherwise.

Two police constables caught her eye and accompanying them was a young, fair-haired man whom she recognised.

Detective Sergeant Joyce of Scotland Yard.

He was the commissioner's son and had controversially replaced Philip in a murder investigation in Westminster. Although he had irritated Augusta at the time, her feelings towards him had warmed a little since then. He was young for a detective, but he had proven himself to be calm and hardworking. She stepped forward to greet him.

'Mrs Peel? This is a surprise.'

'I came here for the fashion show,' she said. 'I accompanied my friend Lady Hereford here. Her niece, Daphne, was the person who discovered the victim.'

'Well, I'm pleased I've bumped into you, Mrs Peel. What are your first impressions?'

'I'm still trying to understand exactly what happened,' she said. 'Lola appears to have been attacked while all the models were on the stage for the final part of the show. The person who attacked Lola must have known she was alone in the changing rooms. I don't know why she wasn't on the stage with everyone else.'

'Interesting.'

'So I think it must have been someone involved with the fashion show. They must have known everybody would go out onto the stage for the finale, leaving few people backstage. It could have been someone helping behind the scenes with clothes and makeup. Another person familiar with the format of the show would be the photographer, Cedric Langley. Lady Hereford and I spoke to him before the show, and I didn't like him. That doesn't mean he's a murderer, of course.'

'No, of course.' Detective Sergeant Joyce smiled. 'But I believe in hunches, Mrs Peel. I think detectives can judge characters quite well. I'll have a word with him. In fact, there will be a lot of people here to speak to, so I'd better get on with it. But if you get any more ideas about this, you'll let me know, won't you? You already have a connection to this case, so you might see or hear something that I don't.'

'If I find out anything else, you'll be the first to hear, Detective.'

She returned to Lady Hereford, who was looking tired.

'Shall we go now, Augusta?'

'Yes.' She took hold of the bath chair and steered Lady Hereford to the exit. Out on Holland Park Avenue, they flagged down a taxi.

The driver was just preparing to pull away when Augusta caught sight of a man waving his arms at the car.

'Is that the detective again?' said Lady Hereford.

Augusta opened the door and Detective Sergeant Joyce jogged up to her, slightly out of breath. 'I'm sorry to trouble you,' he said. 'But I'm having difficulty speaking to Daphne Chatsworth.'

Lady Hereford groaned.

'Every time I try to speak to Miss Chatsworth, her mother answers,' said the detective. 'I've requested to speak to Miss Chatsworth on her own, but she refuses to talk to me without her mother. I'm wondering, Mrs Peel, do you mind very much sitting with Daphne while she speaks to me? Hopefully your presence will reassure them that everything will be alright.'

'I don't mind,' said Augusta. 'But I need to ensure Lady Hereford is accompanied back to her hotel in Russell Square.'

'Don't worry about me, Augusta, I'll be fine,' said Lady Hereford.

'Perhaps you will, but I insist on accompanying you.'

'But you can stay here and help everyone.'

'You need someone with you.'

'May I suggest one of my constables accompanies Lady Hereford in your place, Mrs Peel?' said Detective Sergeant Joyce.

Lady Hereford laughed. 'A police escort! I'm sure I don't need that.'

'But would you mind, Lady Hereford?' asked Augusta.

'No, of course I don't. I'll just go along with whatever makes this easier for everyone. As long as he's handsome, I'm not fussy.'

'I see.' The detective didn't seem sure how to respond to this request. 'I'll see what I can do.'

Chapter 9

A SHORT WHILE LATER, Augusta sat with Detective Sergeant Joyce, Daphne Chatsworth and a police sergeant in a small office at Holland Park Rink. The room had a little desk, a few wooden chairs and a tall cupboard. Photographs of roller skaters and boxers hung in cheap frames on the wall.

'I realise you're extremely upset about what's happened to your friend, Miss Chatsworth. But it's important that we find out what exactly you saw.'

'She wasn't a friend,' said Daphne through tears. She had removed the streaked makeup from her face and changed into an ordinary blouse and skirt.

'Would colleague be a better description than friend?'

Daphne nodded.

'Can you tell me what you saw?'

'I went into the changing rooms and saw her lying on the floor. I thought she'd fainted, so I went over to her. That's when I saw the scarf around her neck. It was pulled tight. So completely, horribly tight!' She buried her face in a handkerchief.

'I know this isn't easy, Miss Chatsworth, but can you recall what happened before Lola was attacked? Did you see anyone running away from the changing rooms?'

She shook her head. 'No, I didn't see anyone.'

'So when the show finished, you were the first model to return to the changing rooms?'

'Yes. All the girls were on the stage for the end of the show and Miss Kingsley joined us. I actually went back to the changing rooms slightly sooner than I should have done.'

Detective Sergeant Joyce raised an eyebrow in interest. 'Why was that?'

'My shoes were so uncomfortable. I had to take them off. But it was only a minute or so before everyone else came back.'

'So you returned to the changing rooms about a minute before the other girls?'

'Yes.'

'Do you know exactly how long?'

'Yes. A minute. It was hardly any time at all.'

'I've had a quick look in the changing rooms and seen all the trunks, cases and racks of clothing in there,' said the detective. 'Do you think it's possible the culprit could have hidden there?'

'What a horrid thought!'

'Do you think it's possible?'

'I suppose it could be. He could have been hiding there. And that could explain why I didn't see anyone running away. He could have still been in there when I found Lola!'

'Possibly.'

'How scary!'

'Did you see anyone acting suspiciously near the changing rooms?'

'No.'

'Was there anyone who seemed out of place? Anyone who you thought shouldn't have been there?'

'No. It was just everyone involved with the show.'

'Tell me who was involved with the show.'

'Obviously there's Miss Kingsley. Then all the models. And a couple of ladies who helped us with our clothes and makeup.'

'Where were the two ladies when Lola was attacked?'

'They were watching the final part of the show when Miss Kingsley went out onto the stage.'

'So they weren't in the changing room?'

Daphne shook her head.

'I'd like to ask a question if I may, Detective,' said Augusta.

'Go ahead, Mrs Peel.'

She turned to Daphne who looked at her with large, mournful eyes. 'Why wasn't Lola on the stage with the rest of you?'

'I think she was probably sulking.'

'About what?'

'She sulked a lot. That's what she was like.'

'Did anything happen this afternoon which gave her a reason to sulk?' asked Detective Sergeant Joyce.

'She had an argument with Sylvia.'

'Did you witness the argument?'

'Yes. We all did.'

'What was it about?'

'It was just Lola being silly. Miss Kingsley made her and Sylvia swap dresses. She thought Sylvia would look better in the pink beaded dress, so Lola had to wear the green dress Sylvia had been wearing and she didn't like it.'

'Does Miss Kingsley often change her mind about who wears which outfit?'

'Yes, all the time! She's made me change lots of times and it doesn't bother me.'

'But it bothered Lola.'

'Yes. After Miss Kingsley made them swap, Lola then tried to persuade Sylvia to swap back again. She said Miss Kingsley wouldn't notice. Sylvia refused and Lola said she didn't want to go out in front of everyone wearing the green dress. I thought she looked fine. She was just making a fuss. And then she sulked because she didn't get her own way.'

'Was it common for Sylvia and Lola to argue?'

'Not really. But I suppose we can all get a bit jealous sometimes. Everyone wants the best outfit, and everyone wants to feel good about what they're wearing. It can be difficult to show the clothes well if you're not comfortable with what you're wearing. I don't think Miss Kingsley should have made Lola and Sylvia swap dresses like she did, but she's the one in charge, so people need to do what she says. If it had happened to me, then I think I would have been annoyed. I can understand why Lola was upset, but she should have just got on with it and walked out for the final part of the show like everyone else.'

'So all the models went onto the stage for the final part of the show,' said Detective Sergeant Joyce. 'And the two women who helped with makeup and clothes went out to watch. Miss Kingsley also joined you all on the stage?'

'Yes.'

'Did she walk onto the stage with everyone else?'

'Yes.'

'Can I add something which I observed?' said Augusta.

'Of course, Mrs Peel.'

'Miss Kingsley walked onto the stage after all the models.'

'So she was last on?' said the detective. He turned to

Daphne. 'Do you know where Miss Kingsley was before she joined you all on the stage?'

'In the changing rooms,' said Daphne.

A pause followed. Detective Sergeant Joyce and the police sergeant exchanged a glance.

'So, just to be certain,' said the detective, 'Miss Kingsley and Lola were alone together in the changing rooms before Miss Kingsley joined you on the stage?'

Daphne nodded.

'How long for?'

'A few minutes. Long enough for us all to walk out there and stand in our places.'

Detective Sergeant Joyce turned to Augusta. 'Would you agree it was a few minutes, Mrs Peel?'

'Yes. That seems about right.'

Augusta wondered if it had been long enough for Vivien Kingsley to attack Lola. Was it possible the fashion designer had been angry about the young woman's sulky attitude? It was difficult to believe she would have murdered her for that reason.

Chapter 10

'I HOPE you haven't been accusing my daughter of anything!' Mrs Chatsworth said to Detective Sergeant Joyce as they stepped out of the office.

'No, I haven't accused your daughter of anything at all,' said the detective. 'I've just been trying to get a better understanding of what happened here this afternoon.'

'You need to catch the man who did this.' She grabbed Daphne's arm and pulled her closer. 'It's unsafe for these young women to be here when there's a murderer on the loose.'

'We're doing all we can to find out the person who did this.' He turned to Daphne. 'Thank you very much for your help, Miss Chatsworth. I realise this isn't an easy time for you.'

'No, it isn't.' She pulled out her handkerchief again and wiped her eyes.

'You probably need to go home and get some rest now, Daphne,' said Augusta. 'You've helped the police a lot this afternoon.'

'You were talking to her for ages,' said Mrs

Chatsworth. 'I don't understand why it had to take so long. Come along, Daphne. Let's get back.' She pulled her daughter's arm and guided her towards the exit.

Augusta and Detective Sergeant Joyce watched them leave.

'Thank you, Mrs Peel, for your help just then.'

'I'm not sure I did much.'

'Yes, you did. Your presence alone was enough to encourage Miss Chatsworth to talk.'

'Hopefully it was useful. I assume you're going to interview Vivien Kingsley?'

'Yes. It looks like she was alone with Lola in the changing rooms. I'll speak to her next and find out what she has to say for herself. Everyone's making a good show of being upset here. But the reality is one of them could be a murderer.'

Chapter 11

'WELL, THAT SOUNDS HORRIFIC,' said Philip when Augusta told him about the murder at the fashion show that evening. They sat in his office drinking tea, although Augusta felt the need for something a little stronger. 'And someone committed the atrocity right under everyone's noses!' he added.

'I don't think many people would have the audacity to do such a thing,' said Augusta.

'No, they wouldn't. This person is brazen and cruel. What have you learned about Lola?'

'Very little. She and Daphne don't appear to have been friends, so I don't think Daphne knows much about her either. Lola had a disagreement with another model when they were told to swap outfits. Lola wasn't happy about what she was wearing and that's the reason why she didn't go on the stage.'

'So the perpetrator must have been close by,' said Philip. 'They must have known Lola wasn't going onto the stage and would be in the changing rooms by herself. What's Daphne like?'

'It's difficult to tell. Lady Hereford told me she was spoiled and prone to whining. I only encountered her when she was very upset about the murder, so she wasn't at her best. Her mother seemed difficult too, but I suspect that's because she was in shock as well. I'd like to meet Daphne again once she's calmed down a little.'

'Could she be a culprit?' Philip asked.

'I can't imagine it. But it's not impossible. She said she left the stage early because her shoes were hurting her feet. I don't know exactly when she left the stage and whether that gave her much time to attack Lola. Even if she had the opportunity to harm her, I have no idea what her motive could have been at this stage. I suppose she has to be a suspect. I feel bad suggesting it because she's Lady Hereford's great niece.'

'At this stage I think everyone who was involved with the show has to be suspected,' said Philip. 'I wonder how Joyce will get on with it.'

'I thought he handled Daphne very well. And I was grateful to him for asking me to be involved in the interview with her.'

'It sounds like he needed you. Did you meet Vivien Kingsley?'

'No. Lady Hereford's niece pointed her out before the show. And then she came onto the stage for the final part of the show to receive everyone's applause. She was the last person to arrive onto the stage at the end. That means she would have been alone in the changing rooms with Lola for a minute or two while everyone else was on the stage. I'm not sure Miss Kingsley had enough time to attack her, but she could have been angry with Lola for not joining in with the final part of the show.'

'Kingsley would have to have a shocking temper if she murdered Lola for that,' said Philip.

'I agree. And as I didn't meet her, I really couldn't say if she's prone to temper tantrums or not.'

Philip sipped his tea as he thought. 'How many models were there?'

'About thirty.'

'And did you see Daphne among them when they were all on the stage at the end?'

'I think so…' Augusta tried to picture them in her mind. 'I can't be completely sure. I remember she was wearing a silver evening gown, and she must have been there. But I can't specifically remember. Isn't memory frustrating sometimes? Maybe Lady Hereford will recall. She has more interest in Daphne because she's a member of her family.'

'It's possible Lady Hereford remembers seeing her. Or maybe Daphne remained in the changing rooms and didn't go out onto the stage at all.'

'No, that couldn't have happened. One of the other models or Miss Kingsley would have seen her there.'

'Good point.'

'But perhaps Daphne hid somewhere,' said Augusta. 'That's a possibility. And if she did, why did she want to harm Lola?'

Chapter 12

Vivien Kingsley had a headache. And the small airless office she was sitting in didn't help.

She closed her eyes and massaged her temples with her fingertips.

'Are you alright, Miss Kingsley?' asked the young detective from Scotland Yard.

'I'm fine.' She opened her eyes to give him and the police sergeant a sharp stare. She needed to get back to her hotel suite and have a lie down. But instead, she had to face the police.

Months of preparation for the show, and this was how it had ended. No one was talking about her latest collection. Instead, they were all talking about the murder.

What a foolish girl Lola had been.

Vivien noticed her hands trembling as she lit a cigarette. If only she could wind back time and start the day again. She longed to live it again with everything going perfectly. She had worked hard to make her show a success. Why had it gone so horrifically wrong?

'How long did you know Lola Parker for?' asked Detective Sergeant Joyce.

'She worked for me for about six months.'

'And how did that come about?'

'I noticed her walking along Kensington High Street and she looked the part. I approached her and asked her if she would like to work as one of my models.'

And what a mistake that had been. She had been attracted to Lola's beauty. The girl had been taller and prettier than all the other girls who worked for her. Before she met Lola, Vivien had employed the daughters of friends as models. All she had looked for was good deportment and an even temperament. But Lola had been different. She looked like one of those sophisticated Parisian girls. From the moment she first set eyes on her, Vivien knew Lola could sell her clothes.

'She'd never modelled clothes before, so there was quite a bit of training involved,' she said to the detective. 'But she was elegant and knew how to carry herself with poise.'

'How many girls do you employ, Miss Kingsley?'

'About thirty. It's rapidly becoming a popular occupation for young, attractive women. I've even had ladies calling on me recently asking if I have any positions available. I have to turn many of them down. I can afford to be choosy these days. A Kingsley girl has to have a certain look about her. And I know it when I see it.'

'What was Miss Parker like to work with?'

Vivien inhaled on her cigarette, choosing her words carefully. 'Spirited,' she said. 'I shan't lie to you, Detective. She was the argumentative sort. However, she was young and not particularly well-bred. She had a lot to learn. In the six months she worked for me, her attitude improved remarkably. It can take a girl a while to realise what standards are expected of her. Lola was getting there.'

'Did she fall out with people?'

'There were disagreements. Lola had strong opinions and that could create discord. I had to have words with her now and again, but I had a soft spot for her. I like people with spirit. Just as long as they do what I say.'

'Did Miss Parker always do what you said?'

The detective seemed quite astute for someone so young. She had to tread carefully. 'Most of the time.'

'And how did Miss Parker get on with the rest of the girls who worked for you?'

'Very well, most of the time. There could be a bit of jealousy now and again.'

'Miss Parker was jealous of the other girls?'

'Jealousy is something which plagues us all. And when everyone's wearing beautiful clothes for shows and photographic sessions, there's always going to be someone envious of someone else.'

'Can you think of anyone who disliked Miss Parker?'

'No. I encouraged the girls to get along with each other and that's what they did most of the time.'

'So you don't know of anyone who could have wished to harm her?'

'No! Absolutely not. And even if one of the girls had disliked her, she certainly wouldn't have strangled her with her scarf. It's unimaginable to picture what sort of monster would have done that to Lola. It certainly would never have been one of the girls. You can rule them all out immediately, Detective.'

'I've heard there was a disagreement between Miss Parker and another girl before the final part of the show.'

Vivien sighed. Who had told the detective that? 'Yes. And that wasn't unusual. It was because I made Lola and another girl swap outfits. Sometimes I like to make changes during the show. I'm a perfectionist. And if something doesn't look quite right, then I change it. I simply asked Lola and Sylvia to swap their outfits because I thought they would look better. Had I known Lola was refusing to go onto the stage, I would have had a strong word with her about it but...'

'But she was murdered?'

'Exactly. The most tragic thing imaginable.'

She inhaled on her cigarette and flicked a speck of stray ash from her black velvet sleeve. It was difficult to believe Lola was dead. She couldn't get the image out of her mind. Her long limbs bent at uncomfortable angles as she lay on the floor.

'When did you find out Lola was refusing to go onto the stage?' asked the detective.

'After she was found.'

'After she died, you mean?'

'Yes.'

Detective Sergeant Joyce sat back in his chair and frowned. Vivien didn't like it. What was he thinking about?

'All the models went onto the stage for the end of the show,' he said. 'Am I right?'

'Yes.'

'You followed them onto the stage?'

'Yes.'

'So you were the last person left in the changing rooms?'

'For a brief moment.'

'Miss Parker was also in the changing rooms, wasn't she? She didn't go out onto the stage for the final part of the show.'

She calmly met his gaze before she spoke. 'I didn't see her.'

He leant forward. 'You didn't see her?'

'No. I had no idea she was still in the changing rooms.'

'But surely you saw her there?'

'No, Detective. I didn't.'

He exchanged a glance with the sergeant which suggested he didn't believe her. Vivien pursed her lips and stared at him.

'Why didn't you see Miss Parker in the changing rooms?' he asked.

'Did you look in there?'

'Yes.'

'Then you would have seen all the boxes, mirrors and racks of clothes there. It was impossible for anyone to have a clear view of the room. I waited by the door for a few moments and then went out to join the girls on stage. Perhaps Miss Parker visited the bathroom while I was waiting. The bathroom is at the far end of the changing rooms, away from the door. Or perhaps she hid from my view, possibly worried I would spot her there.'

'Why would she have worried about that?'

'Because I would have been angry with her.'

'You would have lost your temper with her?'

Vivien thought carefully again before she replied. 'I don't lose my temper, Detective. But I have strong words with people when they're insubordinate.'

Her jaw felt tight with anger. Never before had one of her girls refused to walk out onto the stage! Lola had been rude, disrespectful and completely ungrateful for the opportunity Vivien had given her.

She took in a slow breath through her nose and calmed herself. 'So it's just as well I didn't notice her before I went out onto the stage.'

'Just as well? What do you mean by that?'

'I would have said some sharp words to her, and that

situation was avoided. Anyway, I went out to greet the audience, and they thanked me.'

She smiled as she recalled the adulation. There was no better feeling. Everybody had enjoyed the clothes and the show. At that moment, Vivien had felt sure she would receive a lot of orders from it.

But Lola had ruined it. The girl had sulked and refused to do her job. That decision had cost Lola her life. It had also ruined Vivien's show.

'If Miss Parker had still been alive when you returned to the changing rooms after the show, would you have punished her for her actions?'

'I would have fired her, Detective. A girl only ever disobeys me once. I know it sounds awful saying it because poor Lola is dead now. I'm dreadfully sorry for her family and friends. But I've been affected too, you know. And at this moment, I'm terribly worried about the effect this dreadful murder will have on the reputation of my fashion house.'

Chapter 13

'This has to be the worst day of my life!' said Vivien
Kingsley as she strode into her suite at the Ritz Hotel. She
pulled off her hat and flung it onto a velvet-covered chair.
She dropped her handbag onto an occasional table,
flopped onto the chaise longue, and kicked off her shoes.

'I must look a mess,' she said. 'Pass me my handbag,
would you, darling?'

Nikolai did so, and she took her pocket mirror from
it. As soon as she flipped it open, she wanted to close it
again. Her makeup had sunk into the lines of her face,
emphasising them even more. Her cheeks were flushed
and her nose was shiny. She pulled a lipstick from her
bag and smeared a layer of crimson over her thin lips.
Dissatisfied with the result she saw in the mirror, she
folded it and tossed it with the lipstick onto the deep pile
carpet.

Nikolai offered her a cigarette.

'Thank you.'

'Champagne?' he said as he lit her cigarette.

'Why would I drink champagne at a time like this?

Champagne is for celebrating, Nikolai. What have I got to celebrate?'

The Russian duke walked over to the mirrored drinks cabinet.

'Do they have brandy there, darling?' she asked.

He nodded and poured her drink.

'That poor girl,' she said, once the drink was in her hand. Nikolai sat in a brocade armchair and crossed one long leg over the other. 'I just keep seeing her there, lying on the floor,' Vivien continued. 'I'll never be able to get the image out of my mind.'

'You will.'

'No, I won't! It's not the sort of thing you ever expect to see. And it's all people are going to talk about now. No one's going to remember my show.'

'Of course they will remember it,' said Nikolai. 'It was one of your best shows.'

'That's what I thought. But everyone's going to remember it for the girl who was murdered backstage.'

'They'll catch the murderer soon.'

'How can you be so sure? And anyway, it couldn't have been a man. How could a man get into the changing rooms without being seen? It must have been one of the other girls. Although I refuse to believe one of the girls could have done something like that. I just can't fathom out who else could have done it.'

'Did you see Lola with anyone?'

'No, I didn't. The detective kept asking me the same thing. Why are you asking me questions like a detective, Nikolai?'

'I was only interested to find out if you saw anyone suspicious.'

'No, I saw nothing. I didn't even realise Lola was in there! Isn't that ridiculous? I was too busy worrying about how the show had gone and hoping and praying I would receive some applause when I went out onto the stage.'

Nikolai gave a nod but said nothing more. It frustrated her he didn't know how to comfort her at a time like this. It seemed few men did. Perhaps she was expecting too much from him.

'I really don't know what to do now,' she said. 'We need to start work on the next season, but it looks disrespectful just to carry on, doesn't it? I suppose I shall have to close the business for a few days as a mark of respect. It seems quite ridiculous when you consider Lola was never grateful to me for the job I gave her. In fact, I think she even resented it a little. Such a waste. She was easily the prettiest of the girls, but she was the most difficult. And now look where it's got her. If you're going to be a difficult person, then I'm afraid these things can happen to you.'

'It is sad,' said Nikolai.

'If only Lola had been less disagreeable,' continued Vivien. 'She would have had the world at her feet. She would have been able to do anything she wanted. Beautiful people attract attention, and they can get their own way very easily if they're charming too. But if you're difficult, then people will dislike you very quickly indeed. They'll resent you. It really is possible for a woman to be too much, you know, Nikolai.'

He nodded. 'Yes, it certainly is.'

'I'm not saying I'm perfect, Nikolai. I know I can be difficult. But then I'm not beautiful, am I? I make the best of what I have. But when people meet me, they know what to expect. They don't have other expectations of me.'

'You have to be a determined and clever woman to be a success at what you do.'

'Yes, that's right, Nikolai. And I learned that determination at a young age. I don't bore the girls with my story, but most of them don't have half an idea of what I've been through. I wouldn't change a thing, of course. It made me the woman I am today. But when I see these pampered young things in tears when they've broken a nail...' She shook her head in dismay.

Nikolai was irritating her. He was very handsome, but he was also annoyingly impassive.

'How are you feeling about all this, Nikolai?'

'I think it is very tragic,' he said. 'It's terrible that something bad can happen in a place which you think is safe.'

'Agreed. I'm worried the girls won't want to do any more shows after this. They're going to be terrified, the poor things. I really don't know what to think about it all, my mind's all over the place. And yet your calmness astonishes me, Nikolai. Aren't you at least appalled?'

'Appalled? Yes, I am appalled. It is dreadful. But I didn't know the girl, so I can only feel sad for her.'

'I suppose I know what you're saying, Nikolai. It's just your manner absolutely astonishes me sometimes. I don't know how you do it. I wish I could be like you. Actually, I don't. I like to feel things. I like to express things. You have to be able to do those things in order to create.'

He nodded and inhaled on his cigarette. The man was infuriatingly nonchalant.

'Would you be a dear and run me a bath?' she said. 'I need to do something. I can't just sit here watching you nod your head like a loyal dog.'

Chapter 14

Augusta caught up on her book repairs the following day. She examined a copy of *The Oxford Book of English Verse 1250-1900*. The flyleaf stated the poems had been chosen and edited by Sir Arthur Quiller-Couch. The front cover was almost detached from the spine and some pages at the back were coming loose. Augusta estimated it would take a day to repair, and much of that time would be spent checking all the pages were present.

She found herself reading a few pages. She had almost finished Sir Arthur's preface when there was a knock at the door of her workshop.

'Come in!'

It was Philip. 'I hope I'm not disturbing you, Augusta.'

'No, not at all. Do you know any Greek proverbs?'

'Greek proverbs? Goodness me, no. Why do you ask?'

'Sir Arthur has included some Greek proverbs in his preface. They're written in Greek with no translation. I can work out what the letters are, but I don't understand the actual meaning.'

'What book is that?'

'A book of poems. *The Oxford Book of English Verse.*'

'And you have to understand Greek to read it?'

'No. The Greek is just in the preface. I suppose Sir Arthur wrote his preface with a particular reader in mind.'

'I see. I don't think I'm his sort of reader.'

'You can still enjoy the poems.'

'Good. I'll have a look at them when I have a spare moment. Now, have you had any more thoughts about our plan for meeting the crooked art dealer Mr Briggs? We need to arrange to see him.'

'Yes, we do. How about tomorrow?' said Augusta.

'Tomorrow is perfect.'

'I'll telephone him and tell him I saw his advertisement.'

'Thank you Augusta. Once you've arranged a time with him, I'll tell Morris at the Yard, and he can be close by for when we discover the painting. We'll alert him to it as soon as we leave Briggs's office.'

'And he'll swoop in?'

'Exactly. Now, we need to sort out our cover story.'

'We could pretend to be a middle-aged couple from the suburbs. I'll tell Briggs that I've come into an inheritance, and I want to buy some art with my money. I'll make it clear I know nothing about art, so he'll feel superior and will hopefully enjoy being condescending to me.'

'That's a good idea. We don't want to come across as too knowledgeable or clever, he won't like that. He'll want to be the one in charge. What shall we call ourselves?'

'Stephen and Louisa Dennis.'

Philip nodded. 'Sounds fine. He might ask us where we live.'

'West Norwood. But what if he wants an exact address?'

'We can look up an address in the directory.'

'But if he checks the directory, the name Dennis won't be associated with the address.'

'We tell him we've recently moved house. The directory is only printed once a year, so we'll tell him it's out of date if he brings it up.'

'Good idea,' said Augusta. 'What else shall we tell him about Mr and Mrs Dennis?'

'Mr Dennis is a clerk in an accountancy firm,' said Philip. 'That sounds suitably dull, doesn't it? Hopefully, he won't take much interest in that. And while Mr Dennis is busy working as a clerk, Mrs Dennis is busy keeping house on a sleepy street in West Norwood.'

'It sounds like a peaceful existence,' said Augusta.

'Does it sound preferable to the existence you have now?'

'No. I would be horribly bored keeping house.'

Philip laughed. 'I know you would.'

They heard the ring of the telephone beyond the door. A moment later, Fred appeared.

'Lady Hereford is on the telephone, Augusta.'

She went out into the shop and had barely spoken into the receiver when Lady Hereford began talking. 'Daphne's been arrested!' she said. 'They think she did it, Augusta. They think she murdered that Lola girl. I refuse to believe it.'

Augusta didn't know what to say. She knew there was a possibility Daphne could have harmed Lola, but she could understand why Lady Hereford wouldn't want to consider it. 'I can't pretend my great niece is perfect,' continued Lady Hereford. 'Far from it. She's spoiled and she whines a lot. But she's not a murderer, Augusta. I know that. Can you please have a word with the police and tell them to release her? Better still, ask Mr Fisher to do it. They'll listen to him. He's a former Detective Inspector of the Yard. Ask him to talk some sense into them.'

'But if Daphne's been arrested, that suggests the police have some evidence,' said Augusta.

'Perhaps they do. But the evidence must be wrong. They must be mistaken. I need you to help me, Augusta. Isabella has almost completely lost her mind about this. Will you help?'

It was impossible to say no. 'Yes, Lady Hereford. I will help,' said Augusta.

She returned to her workshop and told Philip.

'Joyce will have a reason for arresting Daphne,' he said.

'That's what I told Lady Hereford, although I don't think she liked hearing it.'

'And it's not surprising. She's a family member. But I can't instruct Joyce to release Miss Chatsworth from custody. I don't have the authority to do that. Even if I had, it would undermine his work. If Daphne is innocent, then she'll be out again very soon.'

'I'll pay her a visit,' said Augusta. 'And see what I can find out.'

Chapter 15

KENSINGTON POLICE STATION stood on Kensington High Street, sandwiched between a gothic church and a public house. It was an attractive red brick building with a large archway running through it and twin gable ends. The lane through the arch led to a court where the town hall, a school and the coroner's court stood.

Augusta arrived there later that afternoon. She had telephoned Lady Hereford to inform her of her plan and arranged to meet Isabella Chatsworth there. She was waiting for Augusta in the reception area. She wore a long olive-green jacket and matching hat. A fox fur coiled around her neck.

'My poor daughter!' she said as a moustachioed constable led them along a wood-panelled corridor. 'How can they bring themselves to lock her up in this place? It's barbaric. She'll never recover from it.'

They met Daphne in a small interview room. The young woman flung herself into her mother's arms as soon as she saw her.

Once mother and daughter had calmed down, they sat

at the table with Augusta. The moustachioed constable stood sentry by the door. 'You're permitted a visit time of fifteen minutes,' he said.

'I'll visit my daughter for however long I like,' retorted Isabella.

Daphne looked despondent. Her hair was flat and her face pale. She wore a plain cotton dress and a grey woollen jacket.

'I don't even know why I'm here,' she said. 'I've done nothing wrong.'

'Mrs Peel is here to get you out again,' said Mrs Chatsworth.

'I can't promise that, I'm afraid,' said Augusta. 'I don't have enough influence with Scotland Yard to persuade them to release you, Daphne.'

'Then what's the point?' said Mrs Chatsworth. 'If you can't get Daphne out of here, then why are you here?'

'I will do all I can to help,' said Augusta. 'And I think it's important for the police to consider other suspects, too. You can help the situation, Daphne, by suggesting other people the police could speak to.'

'This makes sense now,' said Mrs Chatsworth. 'If the police can find someone else to blame for it, then they'll let Daphne go. Is that right?'

'Something like that,' said Augusta.

The constable looked on impassively.

Augusta turned to Daphne. 'What reason did Detective Sergeant Joyce give for arresting you?'

'I was the person who found Lola. That's the only reason!'

'Does he have any evidence?'

'I don't know. And besides, he can't have. I didn't do it!'

'I know you've been asked this already,' said Augusta,

'but can you think of anyone who would have wished to harm Lola?'

'No, I can't. I didn't know her well enough. And it couldn't have been one of the other girls.'

'What about Miss Kingsley?'

Daphne's mouth dropped open. 'Miss Kingsley? You think she could have done it?'

'No, I don't think she could have,' said Augusta. 'But we have to consider everyone who was in or near the changing rooms at the time Lola was murdered. From what I've heard of Miss Kingsley, I really don't think she would have done it. But what do you think? You know her.'

'She would never have done it. Why would she do it?'

'You would know better than me, Daphne,' said Augusta. 'And if you're sure she wasn't responsible and had no motive, then we don't need to consider her anymore. What about anyone else who was there?'

Daphne shook her head. 'It's hopeless. Don't you think I've had plenty of time to think about this? There's nothing else for me to do in this miserable place other than sit here and think about who could have done it.'

'What about Cedric Langley?' asked Augusta.

'The photographer?'

'Yes. Did he and Lola know each other?'

Daphne shrugged. 'I suppose so. I suppose all the girls know him a little bit. But he just takes our photographs. Why would he murder Lola?'

'I just wondered how well you know him. What's he like?'

'He's one of the best fashion photographers there is. He worked in Paris for ten years and he and Miss Kingsley are good friends. We often go to his studio for photography sessions. He's extremely talented at what he does.'

'Did Lola attend any of the photography sessions you did with him?'

'Of course.'

'And how did she get on with him?'

'Absolutely fine, like the rest of us. It's quite simple. All we have to do is stand in the different poses he tells us and he takes photographs. That's all there is to it. I've never had any trouble with him and I don't see why anyone else would. There's no way he would have murdered Lola. Why would he do something like that?'

'That's for the police to find out,' said Augusta. 'But if you think he could be a possible suspect, then we could tell them.'

'He can't be a suspect,' said Daphne. 'He wouldn't have done something like that.'

'But how do you know?' said her mother. 'The person who did this must have been part of the show. Everyone needs to be investigated.'

'I don't want to get Mr Langley into trouble for something he hasn't done,' said Daphne.

'But that's what's happened to you, isn't it?' said Mrs Chatsworth. 'You've been arrested for something you haven't done. There really is no difference, Daphne. I think you should suggest his name to the police just so they'll leave you alone.'

'But what if he finds out I mentioned his name? He won't ever want to work with me again!'

'The police will hopefully consider Mr Langley along with everyone else,' said Augusta. 'I only asked the question because I wanted to find out if you knew of any disagreement he and Lola may have had.'

'No. I don't know anything about that. I wish I did and then I could suggest he was behind this. But I don't think Cedric Langley would have murdered Lola.'

'Did you see him during the show?'

'Yes, he came into the changing rooms shortly before the show began. But I didn't see him after that. He must have been out with the audience taking photographs.'

'Did you see him anywhere near the changing rooms before you walked out for the final part of the show?'

'No. But then I wasn't really looking. I was just thinking about what I had to do.'

'Lola refused to go onto the stage after the disagreement with Sylvia,' said Augusta. 'What's Sylvia like?'

'She's alright,' said Daphne. 'I think it was right that they swapped dresses. She made the pink dress look much better than Lola did. And she was right not to swap back again, even though Lola was pestering her about it.'

'Could Sylvia have murdered Lola?' asked Mrs Chatsworth.

'I don't see why she would have done,' said Daphne. 'And I don't know when she would have found the chance to do it. She was out on the stage.'

'You saw her on the stage for the final part of the show?' said Augusta.

'Yes.' Daphne gave this some thought. 'At least I think I did. I just assumed we were all out on the stage at the end.'

'Presumably Cedric Langley's photographs will confirm it,' said Augusta.

'Of course!' said Mrs Chatsworth. 'We'll soon be able to see who was on that stage and who wasn't.'

'I wasn't,' said Daphne.

'Only at the very end.'

'Yes. But I left the stage early, and that's why the police suspect me. It was all because of those shoes! I couldn't wear them for a minute longer. If only I hadn't had to wear those shoes!'

Chapter 16

AUGUSTA LEFT Mrs Chatsworth bickering with the moustachioed constable about spending more time with her daughter. Although Augusta felt sorry for Daphne, she could understand why Detective Sergeant Joyce considered her a suspect.

To help Lady Hereford, Augusta needed to learn more about the other people involved with the fashion show. She decided to pay a visit to Vivien Kingsley at her fashion house.

Augusta travelled by tube to Bond Street station, hoping to speak to Miss Kingsley before her shop closed for the day. On New Bond Street, shopkeepers were bringing in signs from the street and folding up their awnings. Augusta hurried her step, desperate to reach the Kingsley boutique in time.

She found it close to the junction with Brook Street. Mannequins stood in the window wearing the tea gowns which had appalled Lady Hereford so much. Augusta tried the door of the shop, but it was locked.

A sign on the door displayed the opening hours which

stated the boutique would close at six. Augusta was five minutes early.

Confused, she stepped back to survey the building. She reasoned the Kingsley fashion house occupied much of it for its workshops and offices. It was three storeys high and had attractive sash windows edged with ornately carved stone. Next to the shop was another door. It had no window or number, just a brass knocker. Augusta decided to try her luck and gave the knocker a sharp rap.

It felt like a long wait before the door was opened by a woman in a cotton dress with a white house coat over the top. Augusta guessed she was a seamstress. 'Can I help you?' she said.

'I would like to speak with Miss Kingsley if possible,' said Augusta. 'I'm a friend of Miss Chatsworth's family and I've just visited her at Kensington police station.'

It was enough to persuade the seamstress. 'I'll speak to her assistant,' she said.

A short while later, a harassed-looking woman appeared at the door. She wore a strawberry-red dress with a wide collar and a long drooping silk bow. Augusta repeated her explanation and added that she was a private detective assisting the Chatsworth family.

'Well, I suppose you'd better come in,' said the assistant. She looked about thirty and had mousy, waved hair cut into a fashionable bob. Augusta followed her up a flight of wooden stairs and along a corridor.

'I'm Miss Bilston,' said the assistant over her shoulder as she briskly strode ahead.

'It's nice to meet you, Miss Bilston.'

Augusta caught glimpses of the workshops through open doorways. Rows of sewing machines, long rolls of fabric and wooden mannequins wearing half-constructed clothing. The seamstresses were preparing to leave for the day. Some gave Augusta a curious look as she followed Miss Bilston.

They climbed another flight of stairs and the assistant knocked at a pair of ornate wooden doors.

'What is it?' The voice from within sounded stern.

Miss Bilston gave Augusta a nervous glance before stepping inside and closing the door on her.

Augusta tried to calm her own nerves as she waited. Miss Kingsley seemed to be a formidable woman, and it was possible she would find Augusta's visit an annoyance.

Augusta reminded herself how calm she could be with difficult people. She had encountered people far worse than Miss Kingsley during the war. She mustn't allow herself to be intimidated.

Eventually Miss Bilston reappeared and Augusta was permitted to step into Miss Kingsley's heavily scented apartment. It was filled with furniture, ornaments, mirrors, bookcases and lamps. Oriental rugs lay on the floor and more hung on the walls. There was so much to look at that Miss Kingsley wasn't immediately obvious. Augusta spotted her sitting in an armchair with her shoes lying on the floor close by. Her legs were tucked beneath her and she propped an elbow on the arm of the chair as she held a cigarette in her hand. A stack of bracelets shimmered on her forearm.

'How can I help?' She had sharp blue eyes and her tone was brisk.

'Thank you for agreeing to speak to me, Miss Kingsley. I'm a good friend of Lady Hereford's. Her great niece is Daphne Chatsworth.'

'I see.'

'I run a bookshop in Bloomsbury. But I'm also a private detective.'

Miss Kingsley raised a finely drawn eyebrow.

'Lady Hereford has asked me to help her great niece,' continued Augusta. 'As you probably know, she's been arrested on suspicion of Lola Parker's murder. She wants me to help prove Daphne's innocence.'

'Very honourable of you, Mrs Peel. I don't see how I can help you, though.'

'Do you believe Daphne is innocent?'

'Of course! I was extremely shocked to hear she'd been arrested. I don't understand how anyone could suspect her of murdering Lola. It's simply not possible.'

'The police suspect her because she was the person who found Lola's body. She left the stage shortly before the end of the show.'

'So I've heard.'

'The police presumably think Daphne had time to attack Lola before everyone else returned to the changing rooms.'

'Sounds like nonsense to me.' She inhaled on her cigarette.

'Did you see Daphne leave the stage early?'

'No, I didn't.'

'So you don't know how long she was in the changing rooms with Lola?'

'No.' Miss Kingsley pursed her lips and Augusta sensed she was going to bring the conversation to an end.

'Did you see Lola in the changing rooms before you went out onto the stage for the final part of the show?'

'No. I had no idea she was there.'

How had the designer not seen her? This puzzled Augusta. 'So you thought Lola was on the stage with the other girls?'

'Yes.' Miss Kingsley glanced at the gold watch on her wrist. Time was almost up.

'Photographs,' said Augusta hurriedly.

'I'm sorry?' said Miss Kingsley. 'Photographs?'

'The photographer Cedric Langley was taking photographs of the show.'

'Yes, that's right.'

'He must have photographs of the final part of the show. From those, we should be able to tell how long Daphne Chatsworth was on the stage for during the final part of the show.'

Miss Kingsley rubbed her brow. 'I haven't even looked at the photographs, Mrs Peel. They've not been a priority. One of my girls was murdered at my show. It's all I've been able to think about for these past few days. I've had to close my boutique out of respect for the Parker family and nobody's talking about my collection. All they're talking about is murder. Have you any idea how difficult things are at the moment?'

'I can imagine things must be very difficult, Miss Kingsley.'

'They are.'

'And it's difficult too for Daphne and the Chatsworth family.'

'Of course.'

'I won't keep you any longer, Miss Kingsley. Perhaps I should speak to Mr Langley about the photographs.'

'Yes. Do that.'

'Where can I find him?'

'He has a studio near Kensington Palace. I can't remember the road… just look him up in the directory. You'll find him.'

She gave Augusta a dismissive wave.

Chapter 17

AUGUSTA RETURNED to Kensington the following morning and made her way along streets of large, stuccoed townhouses. Only the wealthy lived here on elegant, tree-lined streets with shiny motor cars parked outside their homes.

She found Mr Langley's photographic studio in Melon Place. It was in a converted stable block in a former mews for the surrounding grand houses.

As she approached the studio, three young women stepped out of the door, chattering excitedly. One of them held the door for Augusta, so she thanked her and stepped inside.

She passed through a seating area with modern chairs and a coffee table piled with magazines and newspapers. A door stood open ahead of her. She peered in to see Cedric Langley in a room with blacked-out windows, a white backdrop screen and a bright spot lamp. He had his back to her as he adjusted his camera on its tripod stand. He was in his shirt sleeves and wore a red satin-backed waistcoat.

'Mr Langley?' she ventured.

'Oh, good grief!' He clasped a hand to his chest. 'You frightened me half to death!'

'I'm sorry I crept up on you,' said Augusta, stepping into the room. 'The door was open. I'm Mrs Peel. We've met briefly before. I was with Lady Hereford at the fashion show.'

His hand remained on his chest as he made a show of recovering his breath. 'I remember. How can I help you, Mrs Peel?'

'I'm a private detective, and Lady Hereford is concerned about her great niece, Daphne Chatsworth.'

'Yes, I heard Daphne had been arrested.' He returned to adjusting his camera. 'Terrible.'

'Lady Hereford has asked me to help prove her great niece is innocent.'

'She is. She would never have done that to Lola.' He shook his head. 'Poor Lola. I still can't believe it.'

'Can you think of anyone who would have wanted to harm her?'

'No. No one.'

'It must have been someone involved with the fashion show.'

'What makes you say that?'

'Because they knew Lola hadn't gone out onto the stage for the final part of the show.'

He smoothed his oiled hair and gave a sniff. 'Well, no one I know would have strangled that poor girl with her scarf.'

'Did you visit the changing rooms that afternoon?'

'Yes, I did. And I know it doesn't sound right that a gentleman would go into the ladies' changing rooms, but I did ask someone to ensure everyone was decent before I went in. I wanted to take some photographs of them all backstage, as it were. After that, I went back into the rink to set up for the show. That's when I encountered you and Lady Hereford. Please do apologise to her again for me asking her to move. If I'd known who she was, I would never have said anything to her.'

'I shall,' said Augusta. 'But I think she's forgotten about it now.'

'I expect she has. It must be very stressful for her with Daphne being arrested. No one likes to think of a family member doing something so awful. And Daphne could never have done it. To strangle someone, you need a bit of strength. Daphne is so terribly slim. And with those little thin arms, I shouldn't think she's got any strength in her to do such a thing.'

'Did you know Lola well?'

He rested an arm on his camera and put his other hand on his hip. 'Not very well. She worked for Kingsley for about six months, I think. I photographed her often, and she was perfectly charming. She could get a little bored, though. Miss Kingsley found her on Kensington High Street one day and I don't think she was entirely suited to modelling clothes. It requires a lot of patience to stand there looking pretty, you know. There are some girls who get along very well with it. And then there are others, like Lola, who look the part but don't possess the qualities needed to do this sort of work. The reality, Mrs Peel, is that it's boring work. And some of our photography sessions can drag on a little. The best girls are the ones with patience. They have to change into outfit after outfit after outfit. And they have to wait while I set up the camera and the backdrop and the lighting. And they have to put up with me telling them how to stand, what to do with their arms, lift their chin, etcetera. All of that.'

'And Lola didn't have the patience?'

'No. Not really. Oh, but she was beautiful, though! The most beautiful girl I've ever seen. And she looked fabulous in photographs. I can understand why Miss Kingsley plucked her from High Street Ken. I would have done the same!'

'What happened when Lola got bored during your photography sessions?' asked Augusta.

'What do you mean?'

'Did it cause disagreements?'

'No, not really. I used to make light of it when she got sulky. I think it annoyed her more than anything, but it was better than falling out altogether.'

'Do you know if she fell out with any of the other models?'

'I simply didn't get involved with any of that, Mrs Peel. Girls will be girls is what I say. And even if she did fall out with one or two, I can't think of a single one who would have murdered her for it! I think you're wrong about the murderer being someone involved with the show. I think it was someone who managed to get in there.'

'It wasn't easy getting into the venue without a ticket.'

'No. So perhaps it was someone with a ticket. Once in there, it wouldn't have been difficult for someone to get into the changing rooms.'

'How would they have known Lola was in the changing rooms on her own?'

He shrugged. 'They didn't. They just went in and she happened to be there.'

'And they strangled her?'

He shrugged again. 'There are some strange people about, Mrs Peel.'

Augusta struggled to believe Lola could have been

murdered by a complete stranger who had happened on her by chance.

'Would it be possible to see your photographs from the show?' she asked.

'Yes, if you want to. I'm not particularly happy with them. That afternoon was a disaster all round, to be honest with you. Come with me.'

He strode out through the door and Augusta followed him to the seating area. 'Have a seat, Mrs Peel, and I'll fetch them for you.'

Mr Langley disappeared through a door at the other end of the seating area and returned a short while later with the bundle of photographs.

'Here you are.'

'Wonderful, thank you.'

Augusta began to look through them. Many of the models and outfits were familiar to her from the show. She spotted Daphne a few times. She was laughing with the other girls in the changing rooms, then she was adopting a serious pose for the stage.

'Which one's Lola?' she asked.

'There.' The photographer pointed to a young woman who stood taller than the others around her. She had dark bobbed hair, sharp cheekbones and large, languid eyes.

'I remember her now,' said Augusta. She recalled how Lola had stood out a little more than the others, and the clothes had appeared to suit her the best.

'Where are the photographs of the final part of the show?' she asked.

'There aren't any.'

'You stopped taking photographs?'

'Not intentionally. My camera broke.'

'Oh.'

With no photographs of the end of the show, it was

impossible to determine when Daphne had left the stage to return to the changing rooms.

'You seem disappointed, Mrs Peel. But not as disappointed as I was on the day. I was furious! The mechanism jammed, and that was that. It's all fixed now, but that's no help, of course. Next time, I shall take two cameras with me.'

Chapter 18

CEDRIC LANGLEY CHECKED his watch as soon as Augusta left. He had enough time before his next appointment.

He put on his jacket, locked his studio and hailed a taxi on Church Street. The distance was short enough to walk in twenty minutes, but he didn't want to get hot and sweaty rushing there.

He gazed out of the window as the taxi passed Kensington Palace Barracks. Mrs Peel unnerved him. Why had she sought him out and startled him like that? How long had she been prowling around his studio without him realising?

She had told him she was helping Lady Hereford prove Daphne's innocence. But she had asked him some odd questions. And why had she wanted to look at the photographs?

For all he knew, she could call on him at home next. And that was why he had to get back there now.

The taxi stopped outside Cornwall Mansions, a row of tall, grand buildings with columned porches. Cedric asked the taxi driver to wait while he dashed into his building.

His flat was on the third floor. His heart pounded with the exertion of running upstairs as he fumbled his key into the lock. Inside, he headed straight for his writing desk and pulled open a drawer. He pulled out the bundle of letters which had been tied up with string. He had kept them just in case he needed them. But now they had to go.

Cedric threw the bundle into the fireplace and retrieved a box of matches from the little Japanese Imari porcelain bowl on the mantelpiece.

He lit three matches in succession, dropping each one on top of the letter bundle. He watched with satisfaction as the paper blackened and curled. Flames flared into life, and the bundle of letters was soon consumed by them.

It took a few minutes before the last of the paper withered and crumbled into small, charred pieces.

The letters were gone now.

Just like Lola.

Cedric smiled. Then he headed back to the taxi.

Chapter 19

'IT ALL SOUNDS VERY PUZZLING,' said Fred when Augusta updated him about the investigation that afternoon. 'From what you tell me, the murderer has to have been someone involved with the show.'

'Yes, it has to be,' said Augusta. 'And two things are puzzling me. Firstly, how could Vivien Kingsley not have noticed Lola had remained in the changing rooms? Once all the models had gone out for the final part of the show, only Miss Kingsley and Lola remained. And yet Miss Kingsley said she didn't see her.'

'You're thinking Miss Kingsley could be the murderer and she's claiming she didn't see Lola there to cover her tracks?'

'It's a possibility.' Augusta thought back to her meeting with the designer. She had struck her as a cold, self-interested person. It wasn't difficult to imagine her losing her temper with a model who had disobeyed her. But could she have murdered her? 'The second thing which puzzles me is Cedric Langley's camera. He has no photographs of the final part of the show because his camera apparently broke.'

'Perhaps he's telling the truth.'

'Perhaps. But if he's the murderer, then it's a convenient excuse for why he took no photographs of the end of the show.'

'I see what you mean,' said Fred. 'But how could he get away with going into the ladies' changing rooms without being noticed?'

'He was the photographer, and he had already visited the changing rooms before the show. I agree that a man wouldn't normally go into such a place, but he had an excuse for doing so.'

'So you think the murderer could be Miss Kingsley or Mr Langley,' said Fred.

'They're definitely suspects.'

'And their motives?'

'Miss Kingsley would have been angry with Lola. And I've heard Lola wasn't very suited to the job. Her refusal to go out onto the stage could have been one of many acts of defiance. Perhaps Miss Kingsley had had enough of her disobedience.'

'And what about Mr Langley's motive?'

'I don't know. That's something I've got no idea about yet.'

The bell above the shop door rang and a bespectacled young woman in a lemon-yellow summer dress stepped inside.

'Hello Harriet,' said Augusta.

Fred grinned and shuffled nervously from one foot to the other.

Harriet greeted them both. 'I enjoyed *Bleak House* enormously,' she said.

'You've finished it already?' said Fred.

'Yes. Isn't Mr Tulkinghorn an interesting character?'

'Yes, very sinister.'

'Sinister! That's an excellent description.'

Augusta checked her watch and realised she needed to get ready for her and Philip's visit to the art dealer, Mr Briggs.

Chapter 20

Mr Briggs's office was in a smart three storey building on Curzon Street in Mayfair.

Augusta stepped out of the taxi and smoothed out the smart blue dress she had changed into for the appointment. Philip relied on his walking stick as he climbed out of the car and joined her on the pavement. He wore a dull tweed suit and spectacles and had combed his hair in a new way. Augusta couldn't resist a smile.

'What's so funny?' he asked.

'You look a little different, but not completely different.'

'A subtle change is enough. Hopefully, I look more like an accountant's clerk than a former police detective.'

'Yes, I think so.'

'Good.'

Philip gave a cursory glance about. 'Morris will be watching us from somewhere. He might be in that van over there with his men. Or maybe they're in one of the buildings overlooking us. Either way, I give them a signal as soon as we leave Briggs's building.'

'What's the signal?'

'I take off my hat with my left hand.'

'And then they'll charge into the building?'

'Yes. And Briggs will be arrested. Exciting, isn't it?'

Mr Briggs received them in a plush office with a thick rug on the floor and a large mahogany desk. He was a portly man with a red complexion and a wave of thick greying hair.

Augusta recalled Detective Inspector Morris telling them Briggs's real name was Fleming. She was amused by the fact all three of them in the office were pretending to be different people.

'Good to meet you, Mr and Mrs Dennis.' He gestured for them to sit on two leather-buttoned chairs.

Augusta reminded herself she was playing a character. She decided Louisa Dennis would be a little more garrulous than her natural self. 'I was expecting to see some art!' She made a point of glancing around the room.

Mr Briggs chuckled. 'This isn't a gallery, Mrs Dennis. I'm an agent. I don't store any of the treasures here in my office.'

Augusta managed to hide her disappointment. She had been hoping she and Philip would have been able to see the painting *Sunset at the Temple Of Artemis*.

'This is merely an introductory meeting for us to find out a little more about each other before we discuss what you might be interested in,' added Mr Briggs.

'Oh,' said Augusta. 'In that case, your advertisement was a little misleading. I was expecting some sort of gallery here. I wanted to look at some art.'

'No, that's not how I work, Mrs Dennis. I pride myself on providing a personal service. I act for several private sellers who choose to remain anonymous. So I'm an inter-mediary, as it were. A go-between. Now, please tell me a little bit more about yourselves.'

'My father died recently.'

'I'm sorry to hear it, Mrs Dennis.'

'Thank you.' She gave a sniff. 'I miss him very much.'

'I can imagine.'

'Since his death, I have come into money,' said Augusta. 'It's no compensation for my loss, but it has helped me a little.'

'I see.'

'And I would like to spend it on something worthwhile.'

'And what better to spend it on than art?'

'That's what I thought.'

'Do you own any art at the moment, Mrs Dennis?'

'Nothing original. Just some prints I bought from Self-ridges department store.'

He gave her a condescending smile. 'And now you have the chance to buy something special.'

'Yes indeed. I've been talking about it for a while, haven't I, Stephen?'

'You have, Louisa,' said Philip with a nod.

'Do you like art, Mr Dennis?' asked Briggs.

'It's not something I know much about.'

'Well, as your wife has expressed an interest in buying art, it's probably a good idea to learn a little more about it.'

'Yes. Quite.'

'So what have you got, Mr Briggs?' asked Augusta.

'As I've explained, Mrs Dennis, I don't have anything here in this building. But my sellers are keen to sell their precious artworks for the right price. My question to you is what sort of thing are you looking for?'

'I like landscapes,' said Augusta. 'I have lots of prints of landscapes at home. A nice large landscape.'

Mr Briggs nodded. 'And you, Mr Dennis?'

'I like whatever my wife likes,' he said. 'It's not a good idea to rock the boat on these matters.'

Mr Briggs chuckled. 'Yes, I understand you. It's the same with me and my wife. It's fair to say she's the one who wears the trousers in our house.' He chuckled again, and Philip joined in. Augusta gave a playful gasp, pretending to be mildly offended.

Mr Briggs rested back in his chair and steepled his fingers. 'I have one or two sellers with landscapes to sell. What sort of price range are you looking at?'

'I have to confess my ignorance,' said Augusta. 'I really don't know much about the price of art.'

'It would be nosy of me to ask exactly how much money you've come into, Mrs Dennis, but as price doesn't seem to be terribly important to you, I can only guess it's not an insignificant sum. Can you give me an idea of what you might be looking to pay?'

'About two hundred and fifty pounds,' said Augusta. The amount was equivalent to what a servant might earn in a year. 'A little more if it's something I really like. But I really hoped I might be able to see some art. If I could see some pictures, then I could have a good idea of how much I would like to pay for them.'

'I absolutely understand you, Mrs Dennis. What I propose at this stage is a second meeting, and what we can do then is discuss the actual pieces of artwork which I think may interest you.'

'A second meeting? I had hoped to buy some art today.'

'I realise that, Mrs Dennis. And I'll readily admit you could walk into any gallery here in London and buy yourself a piece of art immediately. But I offer a unique and personal service. I like to match the artwork to the buyer.

I'd like to learn a little more about the pair of you, because my sellers are quite particular about who they sell to.'

Augusta felt a twinge of discomfort. 'What sort of thing do you want to know?'

'Let me start by making a note of your address.'

Augusta told him the address in West Norwood which she and Philip had agreed on.

'West Norwood is a nice place,' said Mr Briggs. 'So you came in by train this morning?'

'That's right.'

'Did you come into Victoria or London Bridge?'

'Victoria.'

'Of course. It's just a little bit nearer, isn't it? Now tell me, are there any young Dennises?'

'No,' said Augusta. 'Why do you need to know that?'

'It helps give me an idea of the sort of people you are. And I should add that expensive works of art and young children don't mix well. You want to be able to hang a nice piece of art in your home without worrying it will be hit by a ball or covered with sticky fingerprints. How long have you been married?'

'Fifteen years.'

'And I hope you don't mind me remarking, Mr Dennis,' said Briggs. 'But I notice you walk with a stick.'

'Yes. A war injury,' said Philip.

'I'm sorry to hear it. You must have been relieved to return home in one piece.'

'Yes. Something like that.'

'I didn't serve in the war. Asthma.' He patted his chest. 'I was very disappointed because I was desperate to sign up and do my bit. But there you go. At least I tried. Well, it's been delightful meeting the pair of you.'

'Our meeting's over?' asked Augusta.

'Yes, for the time being. Let's meet again in three days'

time and I'll show you some pieces which may interest you. I have to liaise with my sellers first, Mrs Dennis.'

They thanked Mr Briggs and stepped out onto Curzon Street a short while later.

'How do you think that went?' Augusta asked Philip as they walked eastwards towards Berkeley Square.

'Not very well,' he said. 'There was no art to be seen anywhere, was there? And I'm a little worried Briggs is smarter than we thought.'

Chapter 21

'I BARELY KNEW LOLA PARKER,' said Cedric Langley. 'I don't know why you think I can help.'

He placed his hands on his hips as he faced the detective and police sergeant who had called at his studio.

The detective was young and fair-haired and had told him his name was Joyce. He did most of the talking while the sergeant wrote in a notebook.

He didn't like the police here on his doorstep, their presence made him uncomfortable. Even though he found the dark-eyed sergeant quite handsome.

'When did you last see Miss Parker that afternoon?' asked Detective Sergeant Joyce.

'When I was photographing her and the other models during the show.'

'Can you recall what time that was?'

'No, I'm afraid not. I was too busy concentrating on my work.'

'Did you see anyone acting suspiciously at the show?'

'No. But that doesn't mean to say there wasn't. I just wasn't looking out for suspicious characters. I was busy.'

'Did you speak to Miss Parker that day?'

'I don't have any recollection of it. I mean, I may have done. I spoke to a lot of the girls before the show. Lola was obviously there. I don't remember a specific conversation with her, though.'

'Were you aware Miss Kingsley had asked Lola Parker and Sylvia Harper to swap outfits?'

'No, I didn't know anything about that at the time. I've since heard about it and all that occurred in the changing rooms. I didn't witness any of it. Look, I really don't know what you want from me, Detective. I'm as shocked as everyone else about this. It's difficult to believe it's happened.'

'When did you see Lola before the day of the show?'

Cedric thought for a moment. What was the point of these silly questions? There was no use getting annoyed about them because that would antagonise the police. They were probably looking for any reason to suspect people. 'I don't recall the exact dates,' he said. 'It would have been at a photography session here. I photographed the girls in Miss Kingsley's new collection before the show. That took a few days and Lola attended some of the sessions. I forget the exact dates. But everything went well, everyone was polite.'

'I've heard reports Miss Parker was prone to sulkiness.'

'Sometimes she could be.'

'Did that cause a problem for you?'

'Not at all.' He smiled to show how little it had bothered him. 'I'm used to dealing with different temperaments. If a model is sulky during a photography session, then I strike up some entertaining conversation. That always works. I don't actually blame the models for getting a little fed up at times. It can be tedious work. Even the very best models can get tired in a long, arduous photography session. Although it's very glamorous, changing into all those lovely different outfits and having their hair and makeup done, a few hours of it can be quite demanding. I don't think Lola would have done the job for many years. She just happened to look the part, and that's why she was so popular with Miss Kingsley.'

'So her attitude didn't cause any problems for you?'

'No.' He smiled again.

'Did you ever exchange cross words with Miss Parker?'

'As in the Times crossword?' He laughed at his joke and the detective looked puzzled. The handsome sergeant didn't laugh either. 'Oh, you meant cross words. No, there was no need for me to get cross with any of the models. And no cross words with Lola, no.'

The sergeant made more notes and Cedric felt he was doing a good job of persuading them he was telling the truth.

'Can you think of anyone who would have wanted to harm Miss Parker?'

Cedric gave this some thought. He needed the police to focus their attention elsewhere. It was best if he came up with a suggestion.

'Lola fell out with Sylvia Harper shortly before she was attacked.'

'You think Miss Harper is capable of strangling her colleague?'

He shrugged. 'I really don't like to think so. But I don't know Miss Harper very well. She's always struck me as a perfectly pleasant girl. But who knows what comes over some people when they get caught up in a terrible row like that? I'm not saying Miss Harper did it, but sometimes an argument just escalates and escalates and somebody loses their temper. Perhaps they don't intend to kill someone, but they end up doing it by accident. I really don't know if that's what happened to Lola, but it's my best guess for what it's worth, Detective.'

Chapter 22

DETECTIVE SERGEANT JOYCE telephoned Augusta the following day.

'I thought I'd let you know we've let Miss Chatsworth go,' he said.

'She's no longer a suspect?'

'I can't be completely certain about that, but she's no longer in custody.'

'Good.' Augusta knew Lady Hereford would be relieved.

'And I'd like to request your help with something,' continued the detective. 'I've tried speaking to Miss Harper. She's the young woman Miss Parker had an argument with shortly before her death.'

'Sylvia?'

'Yes. The interview didn't go very well. I think she was nervous. Would you mind speaking to her? I think she would prefer talking to a lady.'

'Of course, I'd be happy to help.'

The detective gave Augusta the model's address and,

later that morning, she called at the flat at Montagu Square in Marylebone.

The flat was in a row of tall Georgian townhouses with smart front doors and wrought-iron railings. Sylvia Harper lived in a flat on the top floor overlooking the tree-filled square.

Her mood was cautious. 'I don't understand,' she said. 'Are you working for the police?' She was a tall, dark-haired young woman with pale ivory skin.

Augusta repeated her explanation, emphasising she was a friend of Daphne and Lady Hereford.

'So you're not working for the police?'

'I'm assisting everyone,' said Augusta. 'I'm a private detective.'

'And you mentioned you also own a bookshop.'

'Yes.' Augusta could understand why Sylvia Harper found this confusing.

'This is a lovely flat,' she said, trying to put the young woman at ease. It was filled with antique furniture and old paintings, not the sort of interior Augusta associated with the young woman standing in front of her.

'It's my uncle's flat,' she replied. 'He owns the building. In fact, he owns most of this side of the square.' Her clipped accent suggested a wealthy family and a good education. 'My cousin lives two doors along.' She pointed to a green jacquard armchair. 'I suppose you'd better take a seat, Mrs Peel.'

Miss Harper sank into another chair, sighed, then pushed her bobbed hair behind her ears. She wore a lavender dress with a pleated skirt and a bow at the waist. She looked miserable. Augusta wondered if it was her usual mood or whether it had been caused by her visit.

'My condolences on the passing of your friend Lola.'

'Thank you. She wasn't really a friend. But it was still a shock.'

'How well did you know her?'

'Fairly well. But we weren't friends.'

A pause followed and Augusta left the silence deliberately unfilled.

Miss Harper sighed again. 'I feel like it's all my fault.'

'Why is it your fault?'

'Because if I'd agreed to swap outfits back again with Lola, then she would have walked out onto the stage with the rest of us and the murderer wouldn't have got hold of her.'

'But you couldn't possibly have predicted someone would attack Lola while she was in the changing rooms,' said Augusta. 'No one could have predicted that. Least of all Lola. You followed the instructions which Miss Kingsley had given you. You were happy about it, but Lola wasn't. That doesn't mean you were obliged to go along with her suggestion. I can understand why you feel somehow responsible, but you really weren't. And besides, someone clearly wanted to harm Lola. If they hadn't achieved it at that moment, then perhaps they might have tried another time?'

Miss Harper shuddered. 'It's such a horrible thought.'

'Yes, it is horrible. The police are struggling to understand why anyone would want to harm her.'

'Well, they spoke to me about it, and I felt like they were accusing me.'

'Sometimes it can seem that way. Unfortunately, they're going to consider everyone who had a disagreement with Lola. But it couldn't possibly have been you because you were out on the stage while the attack took place.'

Miss Harper's shoulders relaxed a little. Augusta couldn't be certain the young woman had been on the stage with the other girls at the time of Lola's death. She tried to recall if she had seen Sylvia on the stage at the end, but she had no specific memory of it. And there was no photographic proof either, because Cedric Langley's camera had broken.

'Yes, I was out on the stage when Lola was attacked. But I don't think the police believe me.'

'They probably do. They arrested Daphne, not you.'

'I suppose that's true.' Miss Harper paused. Then added, 'I don't understand why they arrested Daphne. She would never have done it. Who could possibly do a thing like that? I can hardly bear to think of it. They must have just crept up behind Lola and pulled her scarf. She wouldn't have had a chance! It's made me want to stop doing this work. I'm too scared something like that could happen to me.'

'It was a rare incident,' said Augusta. 'And it's unlikely to ever happen again. I can understand why you feel worried now, but I think the murderer planned to attack Lola. No one knows why yet.'

'And that's the horrible thing! If they could just find a reason why someone did this to her, then we could all feel safe again.'

'Can you think of any reasons?'

'No. None.'

'I've heard there were quite a few places to hide in the changing rooms,' said Augusta. 'Apparently, there were racks of clothes and trunks lying about. Do you think it's possible someone could have hidden there without being noticed?'

'I don't know. How would they have got into the changing rooms without being noticed? And I think someone would have spotted them in there before long.

Perhaps someone managed to hide in there and get away with it.'

'It must have been someone with knowledge of the fashion show,' said Augusta. 'And they would have known it would be possible to hide in the changing rooms.'

'I suppose so. I keep thinking about everything over and over. I'm trying to think whether I saw someone who shouldn't have been there. But there really wasn't. And the only other thing I can think of is that one of the girls did it. And I can't bear that thought! I really don't believe one of them would do such a thing to Lola.'

'Can you be certain that Lola was the only girl who wasn't on the stage for the final part of the show?'

'I can't be completely sure. It seemed like everyone was on the stage. In fact, I hadn't even noticed Lola wasn't with us.'

'Did you notice Daphne leave the stage early?'

'No. I was too busy concentrating on my own performance.'

'Was Lola popular?'

Miss Harper twirled a lock of hair with her finger as she thought. 'She wasn't the most popular girl. But she was nice enough. She was different. Miss Kingsley found her on the street. We had a disagreement that afternoon, which everyone knows about. Lola didn't like it when she didn't get her own way, but we usually got on alright together. I can't think of anyone who disliked her or wanted to harm her.'

'What's Miss Kingsley like to work for?'

'She has high standards and is quite demanding. She scares me a little bit. But she has to be like that.'

'Have you seen her lose her temper?'

'Yes, quite a few times. That's because she needs everyone to do what she tells them to. She expects everyone to work as hard as she does. She hates lazy people.'

'Do you know how Lola felt about working for her?'

'I don't think she enjoyed it all the time, she could be quite moody. She liked the clothes, though.'

'What did Miss Kingsley think about Lola's moods?'

'I don't know. But, knowing her, she would have been annoyed by them.'

'So she could have lost her temper with Lola that day?'

'Possibly. She might have lost her temper, but she would never have lost control of herself. If you're wondering if she harmed Lola, Mrs Peel, then you're completely mistaken. She wouldn't have done it.'

'So who do you think did?'

'I don't know.' She gave an exasperated shrug. 'I don't think a woman could have done this. I think the culprit has to be a man. And the only man I saw in the changing rooms that afternoon was Cedric Langley.'

'Could he have harmed Lola?'

'No. Never.'

Augusta got to her feet. 'Well, thank you for talking to me, Miss Harper. If you think of anything else, would you mind letting me know?' She pulled a visiting card out of her bag and handed it to her.

'I will.' She got up to show Augusta to the door.

'There was something else I've remembered,' she said. 'Maybe it's nothing.'

'Even the smallest piece of information can be useful.'

'We had to get to Holland Park Rink for midday. Lola was just ahead of me when I arrived. When we reached the gate, there was a young man leaning against the railings. He called out to Lola, but she didn't respond. It looked like she was deliberately ignoring him. As if he was a nuisance.'

'Have you any idea who he was?'

'No. And I thought nothing more of it. But whether he was annoyed she ignored him and somehow got into the changing rooms…'

'It would be useful to find out who he is. What did he look like?'

'He was quite tall and lanky. About twenty-five. He was wearing a dark suit and a boater hat. There was an expression on his face that I didn't like.'

'In what way?'

'I can't really explain it. But he had an unpleasant look to him.'

'Thank you, Miss Harper. I'd like to find out who he is.'

Chapter 23

BACK AT THE SHOP, Augusta found Fred and Harriet chatting by Sparky's cage.

'Hello Augusta,' said Fred. 'Sparky has just treated us to a song.'

'That's very nice of him.'

'It was lovely,' said Harriet.

Augusta noticed her shopping bag looked full. 'Has Fred sold you more books?'

'Yes he has.' Harriet grinned. 'And I've got *Pickwick Papers* to be getting on with.'

'I hope you enjoy it.'

'I should get on with things. It was nice to see you again, Fred. Bye!'

'Goodbye Harriet.' He smiled as he watched her leave.

'It seems Harriet is becoming quite a regular customer,' said Augusta. 'I wonder why?'

'We sell a lot of good books,' said Fred.

'Is that the only reason?'

Fred turned bashful. 'Of course. Oh look, here's Lady Hereford.' He seemed relieved about the interruption.

'Thank goodness they've let her go!' said Lady Hereford, as her nurse wheeled her bath chair into the shop. 'Daphne's at home now with her mother. Where she belongs.'

'That's excellent news,' said Augusta. 'How is she?'

'Quite fed up about her ordeal. But she's fit and well and she'll recover. Hopefully the police can get on with arresting the right person now. Thank you for all your help, Augusta.'

'I'm not sure that I've done very much. I've spoken to a few people, but I don't think Detective Sergeant Joyce's decision was influenced by anything I did.'

'Oh, you really do talk yourself down, Augusta.'

'I'd like to speak to Daphne again though. Do you think she would be happy about that?'

'Probably not. But only because she enjoys feeling sorry for herself. What do you need to speak to her about?'

'I've learned there was a young man loitering outside Holland Park Rink before the show. He seemed to know Lola. I'd like to find out if Daphne knows anything about him.'

'A young man loitering about? Sounds very suspicious to me. Hopefully Daphne can help. She's at home with my niece, Isabella. They live on Richmond Hill.'

'In Richmond?'

'Where else? Number one hundred and ten. Call on them whenever you're free to do so, Augusta. Hopefully Daphne will be helpful. It's in her interest! She won't want to be arrested again.'

The Chatsworth family home was a large, gold-brick townhouse with double bay windows and a grand cream stuccoed porch.

It was a twenty-minute walk uphill from the train station and Augusta regretted not taking the bus. She had been too impatient to wait for one.

At the top of the hill, the Chatsworth home overlooked parkland sloping down to the winding River Thames. Augusta paused to take in the idyllic view before calling at the house.

'How nice to see you again, Mrs Peel,' said Isabella Chatsworth. 'And thank you for asking the police to let Daphne go. It's been such a terrible time for us.'

'That's quite alright.' Augusta smiled and felt there was little use in trying to explain she hadn't done much. If the Chatsworth family were grateful to her, then she would make the most of it.

Daphne Chatsworth sat in a sitting room with tall windows overlooking the garden. The room was tastefully furnished, and a large vase of white lilies filled the room with their fragrance.

Daphne looked a little better than when Augusta had seen her in the police station. She had waved her hair and wore a peach dress with a white collar and a row of pearly white buttons down the front.

'Everything's been so terrible,' she said. 'I never imagined I'd get caught up in something like this. Just a week ago, I was perfectly happy and everything was normal.'

'Oh how I long for those days again!' added her mother.

A maid served them tea in dainty china cups. The china was so delicate, it was almost translucent.

'Then that awful event happened and everything changed,' said Daphne. 'I can't believe I was kept in a police cell! They shouldn't be allowed to do it.'

'No they shouldn't,' said Mrs Chatsworth. 'Police cells

should be reserved for drunkards and people of the criminal class. Not young women!'

'It's not pleasant,' said Augusta.

'It's cruel!'

'Indeed.' She took a sip of tea and moved the conversation on. 'I spoke to Sylvia Harper yesterday,' she said. 'And she told me about a young man who was hanging about before the show. Apparently he greeted Lola on her way in but she ignored him.'

'Oh, you mustn't believe anything Sylvia says,' said Daphne.

'Why not?'

'Because she's attention-seeking. She says things for effect.'

'Oh? She seemed quite honest to me.'

'Well she's not.'

'I see. Do you remember seeing the young man when you arrived at the show? Sylvia told me he was leaning against the railings.'

'No. I didn't see him.'

'Do you know who he could have been?'

'No idea.'

'Do you know if Lola had a boyfriend?'

Daphne paused for a moment, as if giving this a lot of thought. Then she cleared her throat. 'There was someone called Eddie, I think.'

'Did you meet him?'

'I didn't actually meet him. But I saw her with him once or twice.'

'What did he look like?'

'I can't really remember. Quite thin. Tall.'

'How old was he?'

'I don't know. Twenty-something.'

'Do you know anything more about him?'

'No, nothing.'

'Do you know anyone who might?'

'You could ask Lola's flatmate, I suppose. She might know.'

'Do you know her flatmate's name?'

'No.'

Chapter 24

'Oh, I just want to be left alone!' said Daphne after Mrs Peel had left.

'She's a nice lady. She helped you,' said her mother. She perched on the arm of Daphne's chair and affectionately smoothed her hair. It felt irritating. Daphne shook her head free.

'I know she helped me and I'm grateful. But I'm tired of having to think about it and talk about it.'

'Hopefully you won't anymore. It sounds like that young man had something to do with it.'

'Eddie? Maybe. But I don't remember seeing him at the show. And how would he have got into the changing rooms?'

'He must have sneaked in while no one was looking.'

'While the show was on?'

'Yes. When else?'

Daphne considered this some more. 'And he could have hidden in there, couldn't he?'

'From what you've told me, it was very cluttered in there with lots of clothes and cases and so on.'

'I suppose it makes sense. Lola probably ended it with him and he was angry about it.'

'So he sought revenge.'

'How horrible!'

'I'm afraid we live in a horrible world, darling. That's why I'm pleased you're safe here at home with me.' She patted Daphne's arm and got to her feet. 'I don't want you doing work as a model anymore. It's too dangerous.'

Daphne felt a twinge of indignation. 'No, it's not! This happened because Lola's boyfriend attacked her. That's nothing to do with being a model. I don't want to stop working for Miss Kingsley!' She liked the clothes too much. And she enjoyed looking beautiful and receiving attention. Fascinating, handsome people took an interest in her these days. 'I won't stop it,' she added.

'Well, I shall have to see what your father thinks about it all. If he forbids it, then you must do as he says. And if you're sure this boy called Eddie is the murderer, then you must tell the police about it. It's not fair that you were the one locked in a police cell while he's wandering about as free as a bird.'

'Can't you telephone the police, Mother? I can't bring myself to speak to them ever again.'

Chapter 25

AUGUSTA WALKED BACK down the hill and found the Richmond-upon-Thames post office. It was a grand red-brick building with a stone-carved coat of arms above the doorway. She used the public telephone inside the post office to telephone Detective Sergeant Joyce.

'Eddie?' he said after she had told him about her conversation with Daphne. 'Do you know his surname?'

'No. But I'm hoping Miss Parker's former flatmate might know.'

'Ah, yes. Mabel Roberts.'

'Have you spoken to her?'

'Yes, but she didn't mention a young man called Eddie. If you could find out more from her, Mrs Peel, I would be grateful.' He gave her an address in the Bourne Estate in Holborn.

It was early evening when Augusta arrived at Lola's former flat. The Bourne Estate was a large complex of modern apartments which had been built for workers. The contrast with the homes Daphne and Sylvia lived in was startling.

There were six or seven blocks, and it took Augusta a while to find the address. Eventually she called at the door of the fourth floor flat.

Mabel Roberts looked reassuringly ordinary when she opened the door. She wore a blue cotton dress and her wavy hair looked a little unkempt, as if it had been neglected during a day at work. She looked like a shop girl or a waitress.

'Come in,' she beckoned Augusta through a narrow hallway and into a small, comfortable sitting room. She listened intently as Augusta explained who she was and why she was there. And she accepted Augusta's condolences with a grateful nod.

'I still can't believe Lola's gone,' she said.

'How long were you friends for?'

'About three years. We worked at Goldings together.'

'Goldings?'

'You don't know it? Sorry, I should have explained. It's a stationer's on Gray's Inn Road. We supply a lot of the law offices.'

Augusta knew Gray's Inn was close by. It was one of the four inns of court for barristers.

'Lola left Goldings when she went to work for Miss Kingsley?'

'That's right. That was about six months ago.'

Mabel sat forward in her chair, keenly engaging in the conversation. Augusta could tell she was eager to help. She hoped this meant Mabel was truthful, too.

'Did Lola enjoy her work for Miss Kingsley?' she asked.

'Some of the time. She loved wearing the clothes. And who wouldn't?' She smiled. 'She liked having her hair and makeup done, and she was proud of the photographs they took of her. I was a bit jealous, to be honest with you. It looks lovely getting dressed up like that and being paid for it. But there's no chance of me getting a job like that!' She laughed.

'I think you're being unkind to yourself,' said Augusta.

Mabel laughed again. 'She was tall, thin and very beautiful. And I'm the complete opposite!'

'Beauty is in the eye of the beholder. Isn't that how the saying goes?'

'I suppose so. But Lola was very beautiful. When I saw the photographs they took of her, I told her she looked like a proper lady!'

'Do you know much about Lola's family?'

'She didn't really have any. She didn't know who her father was, and her mother died about five years ago.'

'So Lola relied on her salary from the shop to get by?' asked Augusta.

'Yes. But she earned a lot of money when she began working as a model for Miss Kingsley.'

'Really?' Augusta recalled Lady Hereford's niece mentioning Miss Kingsley paid her models five pounds a week. She imagined Mabel Roberts' salary was similar.

'Yes, she bought herself lots of fancy things with it. New outfits and trinkets for her room.' She paused and compressed her lips. 'I miss her.' She took a handkerchief from her sleeve and wiped her eyes. 'She was a good friend.'

Augusta waited while she composed herself again.

'Thank you for talking to me about Lola,' she said. 'I realise this isn't easy. I never met Lola, but from what you tell me about her, she seems to have been an ordinary girl. Many of Miss Kingsley's models are from aristocratic families. Did Lola ever mention that?'

'Yes, she told me they were all posh. I think she had a few snobby comments from them.'

'Did that upset her?'

'Yes. But I think she tried to ignore it the best she could. In fact, she tried to change her ways a bit.' Mabel gave a little laugh. 'She put on airs and graces that she hadn't done before. I laughed at her for it, and she saw the funny side too. She behaved like that because she wanted to be like the other girls. She never felt like she fitted in with them all.'

'Do you know who Eddie is?' asked Augusta.

Mabel rolled her eyes. 'He was Lola's boyfriend for a bit.'

'The relationship was over at the time of her death?'

'Yes, it had been over a few months by then.'

'What did you think of him?'

'I didn't like him much. He wanted to have too much control over her. Always wanting to know where she was going and who she was with. She got fed up with him.'

'She ended it?'

'Yes. He took it badly.'

'What did he do?'

'He kept coming round here all the time! He was a nuisance.' It made sense to Augusta why he had been hanging about outside the fashion show. He had wanted to speak to Lola, and it seemed she had done her best to ignore him.

'Do you know his surname?' Augusta asked.

'Miller. He wanted to get back with her again. But that was never going to happen because I think there was another boyfriend. But she was all secretive about him.'

'What makes you think there was another boyfriend?'

'She would get all dressed up and go out for the evening. Sometimes she would tell me who she was going out with, and sometimes she would just give a coy smile and tell me not to wait up for her.'

'Why do you think she was secretive?'

'Maybe she was seeing someone who was married. Although she did say Eddie would be angry if she ever had another boyfriend.'

'She worried about that?'

'Yes, I think she did. She once said to me, "If I meet someone else, Eddie must never find out. He'll be furious about it."'

Augusta already felt a strong dislike for Eddie Miller. 'Was Lola scared of him?'

'Maybe a little bit. She just didn't want any trouble from him.'

'Does he have a job?'

'Yes, he works at the new Lyons factory out at Greenford.'

'I know the one you mean.' It was a vast, modern factory which produced tea and coffee. 'Perhaps I shall call on him there.'

Mabel blew out a sigh. 'Good luck, Mrs Peel. He's a strange fellow.'

Chapter 26

Augusta telephoned Detective Sergeant Joyce the following morning and told him about Eddie Miller.

'I'm surprised Mabel Roberts didn't tell me about him when I spoke to her. I asked her if Lola had a boyfriend.'

'Eddie is a former boyfriend.'

'I suppose that explains it then. It's important to be thorough in the wording of your questions, isn't it? It sounds like a trip to Lyon's in Greenford is in order. Would you like to accompany me, Mrs Peel?'

Augusta replied that she would. An hour later, they boarded the train together at Paddington railway station.

'Thank you for your help so far, Mrs Peel,' said Detective Sergeant Joyce as he settled into his seat. 'I'll make sure you're reimbursed for your work.'

'I'm not doing this for the money,' she said. 'Lady Hereford asked me to help.'

'And you're a great help. You have a knack for extracting information from people. It must be the woman's touch. It's a shame the Yard can't employ you as a detective.'

'I prefer running my bookshop.'

He smiled. 'I think you like the excitement of each case as well.'

'Yes, I suppose I do. It keeps my mind active.'

The train pulled out of the station and began making its way through drizzly west London.

'I was wary of you when I first met you, Mrs Peel. Probably because I didn't quite understand you. I couldn't fathom why a lady who sold and repaired books was also a detective. And I was also confused about your relationship with Mr Fisher.'

'That's understandable.'

'But you appear to be someone who loves books and also has a good mind for solving cases. And you and Mr Fisher worked together during the war.'

'We shared many experiences,' said Augusta. 'Good and bad.'

'I can imagine,' said Detective Sergeant Joyce. 'I wish I'd been able to do more for the war effort.'

'You were a young police constable, and you were needed here in London.'

'That's one way of looking at it.' He turned to the window where the suburbs rolled past. 'I would like an opportunity to prove myself. Everyone who served in the war was given that challenge. And many paid the ultimate price. I'm lucky and I've been given this opportunity by my father. But the fact he's the commissioner means my colleagues don't always take me seriously.'

Augusta was reminded of the commissioner replacing Philip with his son. It had angered her enormously at the time. 'I suppose most people are used to you by now though, aren't they?' she said.

'I suppose so. It's not easy work, and there are many things which keep me awake at night when I'm working on a difficult case. But hopefully my colleagues are realising I can do the job. Plenty of them wanted me to fail.'

'Well, you've proved them wrong.'

As the train pulled into Greenford, Augusta saw the vast Lyons factory stretching out to her right. The factory occupied a section of land between the canal and the railway line and was a modern building of smart red brick with rows of grey pitched roofs.

The area had been rural before the war, but houses were now being built close to the factory. Augusta guessed the surrounding green fields would be gone before long.

She felt spots of rain on her face as she walked with Detective Sergeant Joyce along the tree-lined road leading to the factory.

'It's some operation they've got here, isn't it?' he said. 'I read about this place in the newspaper. They bring the coffee and tea along the canal from London's docks each day. Then they process and package it all here and send it back out again by rail.' He pointed to where a train stood in a siding at the factory's railway depot.

An aroma of coffee hung in the air and Augusta was impressed by how much cleaner the factory was than the smoky, dirty industry in the centre of London.

At the main office, Detective Sergeant Joyce showed his warrant card to a smart young woman behind a desk and asked if he could speak with Eddie Miller. She said she would see what she could do and dashed off, eager to help.

A few minutes later, a middle-aged stocky man arrived at the office with a lanky young man wearing a cap and overalls. Augusta recalled Sylvia Harper's description of Eddie and how she hadn't liked his expression. Augusta realised what she had meant now. His eyes were pale and hooded, and there was a trace of a sneer on his lips.

His stocky companion introduced himself as Mr

Henderson. 'May I ask what you want with this young man, Detective?' he asked.

'I have a few questions for him regarding Miss Parker.'

'And who's she?'

'She's the young woman who was murdered at the Kingsley fashion show a few days ago.'

The man's face paled. Then he turned to Eddie and looked him up and down. 'Good grief, young man. Did you do it?'

'Please allow me to ask him the questions, Mr Henderson,' said Detective Sergeant Joyce. 'Mr Miller's not a suspect at the present time. We just need him to help us.'

'I see.' Mr Henderson seemed relieved by this news. 'Very well. Take all the time you need, Detective.' He turned to the young woman who had now reappeared behind the desk. 'Show them to the meeting room please, Miss Watkins.'

The carpeted meeting room had a shiny table with a dozen chairs. Framed advertisements for Lyons and photographs of their corner house establishments hung on the wall.

Eddie Miller sat facing Augusta and Detective Sergeant Joyce. His arms were folded and his expression was defiant.

'How long did you know Lola?' asked the detective.

Eddie shrugged. 'About a year.'

'And did you know her well?'

'Very well. We courted for a while. But then she moved on.'

'Moved on to where?'

'Don't know. She wanted nothing to do with me anymore.'

'Did you have a disagreement?'

'Not really. I think she just got bored with me and found someone else.'

'So she went off with someone else?' asked Detective Sergeant Joyce.

'I don't know. I asked her for an explanation, but she wouldn't give me one.'

'So she told you she wanted to end the relationship but didn't give you a reason?'

'Yes. She said it was over and she didn't want to talk about it any more than that.'

'How did you feel about that?'

'It wasn't what I wanted to hear.'

'Did you try to change her mind?'

'A few times. But it didn't work.'

'You think she met someone else?'

'I think so.' He rubbed at his face. 'I asked her and she denied it. But she was probably lying.'

'No one has mentioned she had a boyfriend,' said Detective Sergeant Joyce. 'Have you any idea who the other person was?'

'No. But it must have been someone in her new world.'

'New world,' repeated Augusta. 'Why do you describe it as that?'

'Because everything changed when she started working in that new job.'

'You knew her when she was working at Goldings?'

'Yeah, that's where I first met her.'

'And she changed when she began working as a model?'

'Yeah. And she had men looking at her. I didn't like that.'

Augusta suspected he was jealous.

'Did you see Lola again after she ended your relationship?' asked Detective Sergeant Joyce.

Eddie nodded. 'A few times.'

'You arranged to meet each other?'

'No, we didn't arrange nothing. I just called on her when I was passing by and said hello and asked her how she was doing. That sort of thing.'

'And did she mind that?'

'I don't think she minded. And anyway, I was only being friendly. I don't like falling out with people. I like to stay friendly with everyone.'

'Did she tell you to stay away from her?' asked Augusta.

'No. Why would she do that?'

'When did you last see her?'

'A few weeks ago. Near her flat.'

'Did you deliberately go there?' asked Detective Sergeant Joyce.

'I was walking nearby and then I noticed I was near her flat, so I walked past the building and I happened to see her coming out.' Augusta suspected he had been waiting for her there, just as he had been waiting for her outside Holland Park Rink. 'Did you speak to her?' she asked.

He nodded. 'Asked how she was and what she was up to. That sort of thing.'

'Was she happy to see you?'

'Difficult to tell.'

'Did she smile at you? Ask you any questions about yourself?'

'She told me she was busy and had to get on.'

Augusta suspected Lola hadn't been pleased to see him and that he had been making a nuisance of himself.

'And that was definitely the last time you saw Lola?' asked Detective Sergeant Joyce.

'Yeah.'

'A colleague of Lola's said she saw you outside Holland Park Rink on the day of her death.'

Eddie said nothing, then rubbed his face.

'Thinking about it… I was there then. I'd forgotten about that.'

'Did you see her that day?'

'Yeah, I saw her going into the show.'

'How did you know she would be there?'

'I saw the advert for the show and I guessed Lola would be part of it. I couldn't afford a ticket, but I thought I'd wait outside and wish her luck as she went in.'

'And did you speak to her?' Augusta asked, knowing the answer.

'Yeah, but she was in a hurry. She said hello, and that was it.'

'Her colleague seems to think she deliberately ignored you.'

Eddie scowled. 'Who said that?'

'One of the girls she worked with.'

'Then you can tell her that's wrong! Lola said hello to me!'

'Did you go into the show?' asked the detective.

'No. I didn't have a ticket.'

'Did you find a way in without a ticket?'

'No! I didn't go in!'

Chapter 27

'I'm afraid Sparky has been misbehaving,' said Philip when Augusta returned to the shop. He stood by the counter with Fred. 'He's been singing so loudly that he disturbed my work.'

Augusta smiled. 'Don't tell Lady Hereford, she'll be cross with him.'

'I won't tell her this time. But I've warned him if he sings that loudly again, then I'll have to report him.'

'I hope he heeds the warning,' added Fred.

'How was your excursion with Joyce?' Philip asked Augusta.

'It was quite interesting. We spoke to a man called Eddie Miller, a former boyfriend of Lola's.'

'And what's he like?'

'Odd.' She told him about the conversation. 'I don't think he was telling me the complete truth,' she added. 'And I suspect he was more upset about the breakup of his relationship with Lola than he wished to admit. It explains why he kept trying to see her.'

'It's not uncommon,' said Philip. 'Some people struggle

to accept the end of a relationship and Mr Miller sounds like one of them.'

'I'd like to visit Holland Park Rink again and work out if Eddie Miller could have got in there without being seen.'

'Sounds like a good idea. I'd like to come with you and have a look at the place myself,' said Philip. 'I'll telephone the place and see if there's someone there who can let us in.'

That afternoon, Augusta and Philip headed for the British Museum tube station from where they could travel by the Central London tube line to Holland Park. A light drizzle fell as they walked through Bloomsbury Square.

'Eddie Miller thinks Lola Parker would have met someone else,' said Augusta. 'And that's why she ended their relationship.'

'But he doesn't know who the person is?'

'No. And Joyce said no one else has mentioned she had a boyfriend. Lola's flatmate, Mabel, told me she suspected Lola was meeting someone else, but she never confirmed it.'

'So it sounds like there could have been a secret relationship which few people knew anything about. Have you any idea why Lola was so secretive about it?'

'Apparently, she told Mabel that if she had another relationship, she didn't want Eddie to find out. She told Mabel he would be furious about it. Mabel said Lola didn't want any trouble from him.'

Philip shook his head. 'The behaviour of this Eddie chap is concerning. He may be little more than a nuisance, but men who behave like that sometimes have sinister intentions. One can't underestimate the effect rejection can have on some people. They can struggle to accept it and may even seek revenge.'

At Holland Park Rink, a man in overalls unlocked the door for them.

'You said you'd be here at three,' he said.

'Yes.' Philip checked his watch. 'And it's only five minutes past.'

'You need to be quick. The ladies' roller-skating club will be here at half past.'

'Very well.' They stepped into the dingy interior. 'Please can you put some lights on for us?'

The man grunted and disappeared from view. A moment later, the lighting flickered on, illuminating the shiny wood floor and empty galleried seating. A curious odour lingered in the air, a combination of polish, old newspapers, and stale sweat.

Augusta gave a shiver. 'There's something spooky about large, empty buildings.'

'Yes, I know what you mean,' said Philip.

'It looks very different now. It's hard to imagine the fashion show was held here.'

'Let's find the changing rooms.'

They followed a corridor which ran behind the lower tier of seats. Eventually they reached a blue door with a sign declaring it was the ladies' changing rooms.

Augusta felt a prickle on the back of her neck. This was the place where Lola Parker had lost her life. She didn't like the thought of going into the room.

'You'll need to check there's no one in there before I go in,' said Philip.

'Of course there'll be no one in there.'

'I'd like you to check first.'

'Alright.' Augusta pushed open the door and stepped inside. The electric lighting was weak. The floor was tiled, and low wooden benches ran along the pale-yellow walls. Daylight filtered through the opaque glass of small rectangular windows high in the walls. Above the benches were rows of hooks. A pair of shabby plimsolls hung from one of them.

A yellow door at the end of the room stood ajar, from beyond it a steady drip of water echoed. Augusta made her way to the door and peered through it to see two empty lavatory cubicles, a little window and two basins. She wrinkled her nose at the sour smell and went back to Philip to tell him it was alright to enter.

He was even less impressed with the room than she was.

'It's got an odd feeling about it, hasn't it?' he said.

'Probably because we know what happened here.'

'Yes. But the fact this was used for a fashion show… it seems so at odds with Miss Kingsley's luxurious clothing.'

'I agree. I'm trying to picture how busy it must have been at the time of the show,' said Augusta. 'Apparently racks of clothing had been wheeled in here, and they had set up some makeshift dressing tables and mirrors. It must have been quite cluttered and fairly easy for someone to hide.'

'So let's imagine Eddie Miller got in here,' said Philip. 'He couldn't have climbed in through the windows, they're too small. He had to have got in through the door. The changing rooms are easily accessible from the seating area, but I don't see how a man could have walked in here without being challenged. I'm assuming there are lavatories beyond that door at the far end.'

'Yes. And there's only a little window in there too.'

'Mysterious,' said Philip. 'Let's continue looking around.'

They left the changing rooms and continued along the corridor until they reached the gentlemen's changing rooms.

'These ones weren't used for the show, were they, Augusta?'

'No, only the ladies' changing rooms.'

'I'll have a quick look inside anyway, but I'm not expecting to find anything useful.'

Augusta waited until Philip reappeared.

'Just as I thought,' he said. 'Nothing.'

They continued on to where the corridor ended and there was access to the rink side seating and the rink via a little gate.

Philip stopped and leaned on his walking stick as he turned to look at the route they had just taken. 'So the models came out of the changing room and walked along this corridor before going through the gate and onto the stage?'

'Yes, that's the quickest route. And I recall there being some steps just beyond the gate so they could climb up onto the stage.'

'So let's imagine they're all out on the stage for the final part of the show. If Eddie had got into the building, then he could have taken that opportunity to go into the changing rooms and attack Lola Parker.'

'But how would he have known she was in there?'

'Because she wasn't on the stage.'

Augusta nodded. 'But he would've had to have got out of the changing rooms without being seen too.'

'Perhaps he did. Perhaps he was exceptionally lucky to not be seen both times.'

Chapter 28

AUGUSTA AND PHILIP walked up to the little gate. Augusta lifted the latch on the gate and swung it open. They stepped out onto the shiny rink floor.

'If I had been a model here that afternoon,' said Philip, 'then I would be walking onto the stage now.'

Augusta smiled. 'Yes. And you'd have made a very good model.'

'Thank you.'

They stood at the top of the rink where the stage had been.

'There was a walkway leading out from the stage into the middle of the rink,' said Augusta. 'There were chairs set around it and they were all full. The rink side seats were all full too, as was the upper gallery.'

'And where were you and Lady Hereford sitting?'

'About there.' Augusta pointed to a spot slightly ahead and to her left.

'So you weren't in a position to see what was happening near the changing rooms,' said Philip.

'No, we were nowhere near them.'

'It's possible Eddie Miller got into the building and went into the changing rooms during the final part of the show,' said Philip. 'Let's think about the other suspects though. What about Miss Kingsley?'

'She could have been angry with Lola for refusing to go onto the stage,' said Augusta. 'We know Lola was sulking because she didn't like the outfit she was wearing. Miss Kingsley could have ordered her to go onto the stage, and she could have refused. We know Miss Kingsley can lose her temper because Sylvia Harper told me that. Miss Kingsley may have lost her temper with Lola that afternoon and tugged her scarf tight. She may not have intended to kill her or even hurt her. But it's possible she got carried away.'

'Miss Kingsley claims she didn't see Lola in the changing rooms, didn't she?'

'Yes. And having seen the changing rooms now, I don't believe her. Even though it was cluttered in there, I can't see how she would have missed Lola.'

'So it's rather convenient for Miss Kingsley to claim she didn't see Lola. If she admits to it, then we'll assume she was angry with her and lost her temper. What did Miss Kingsley do when she joined the models on the stage?'

'She bowed and thanked the audience for their applause.'

'And how did she look?'

'Rather happy to be the centre of attention. She certainly didn't look like a person who had just strangled someone.'

'It would be quite an accomplishment to appear on stage like that after having just committed a murder. It's not impossible, though. Miss Kingsley is a strong suspect. And her claim that she didn't see Lola in the changing rooms is baffling. I suspect it's a lie. But there may be another reason she's lying about it. What about Sylvia Harper? She fell out with Lola Parker, didn't she?'

'Yes, they had a disagreement after Miss Kingsley made them swap outfits. Lola asked Sylvia to swap back again, but she refused.'

'So Sylvia could also have murdered Lola out of anger,' said Philip. 'But to do that, she would have had to remain in the changing rooms with Lola or leave the stage early as Miss Chatsworth did.'

'We have no evidence she did either.'

'It's a shame Cedric Langley the photographer didn't get any photographs of the final part of the show,' said Augusta.

'Yes, it's a shame and also rather suspicious,' said Philip. 'Did his camera actually break? Or does he have no photographs of that part of the show for another reason?'

'We don't know where he was at the time of Lola's murder,' said Augusta.

'He could have noticed Lola hadn't joined the other models on the stage and gone into the changing rooms when she was in there alone,' said Philip.

'I think he had the opportunity to do it, but I don't understand what his motive could have been.'

'We need to learn more about that man. And even though Joyce released Daphne from custody, it doesn't mean she's innocent. I think she could have had time to leave the stage, get back to the changing rooms and attack Lola. How long does it take to walk from here to the changing rooms? Twenty seconds? Half a minute at the very most I'd say.'

'I agree,' said Augusta.

'But there's still Eddie to consider too. Let's look around a little more and see if there are any other sneaky ways into this place.'

They left the rink and returned to the corridor which had led them past the changing rooms. They followed a new corridor which led behind the top of the rink. There were several doors, and they tried each one.

The first door opened into a workshop which had a workbench and shelves of roller skates. There was a store-room with mops, brooms and buckets. Then there was a windowless office with a desk, a few wooden chairs and a cupboard. Photographs of roller skaters and boxers hung on the wall.

More doors led to more lavatories. Then they reached a small area with a counter for serving tea and coffee. The chairs were stacked on top of the tables. It looked rather sad and empty.

Augusta spotted something in the far corner. 'There's another door,' she said.

'So there is,' said Philip. They stepped over to it and tried the handle but it was locked.

'There's daylight beneath the door,' said Augusta. 'It must lead outside.'

'I wonder if it's always kept locked. The grumpy care-taker should be able to tell us.'

'I suppose it's another way Eddie could have found his way in,' said Augusta. 'I can imagine there was a demand for tea and biscuits during the fashion show. If this area was busy at the time, then he could have come in through the door and I don't think many people would have paid him much attention.'

'How would he even know the door was there?'

'Perhaps he decided to try his luck and walk around the building,' said Augusta.

'So Eddie Miller loitered outside, hoping to speak to Lola,' said Philip. 'She ignored him when he greeted her and that probably made him angry. He would have found it difficult to get in through the main door because they were checking tickets. So he walked around the building to find another way in. He found this door unlocked, and he walked through the cafe area without drawing much attention to himself. All he had to do then was follow the corridors until he found the ladies' changing rooms.'

'Then he waited until everyone was on the stage before he went in there.'

'And he went in there because he noticed Lola was missing from the stage. She wouldn't have been happy to see him. Perhaps she was rude to him and he didn't like it?'

'It sounds possible,' said Augusta. 'But only if Eddie managed to get into the building that afternoon.'

'Joyce and his men need to speak to everyone who was at the fashion show,' said Philip. 'It won't be an easy task, but they need to find someone who saw Eddie Miller here. If he got into the show through the cafe door, then someone must have seen him walk in here. I'll have a word with Joyce and see what he thinks about the idea. In the meantime, we need to get ready to see Mr Briggs again tomorrow.'

'He had better have the paintings with him this time,' said Augusta.

Chapter 29

'How DELIGHTFUL IT is to see you again, Mr and Mrs Dennis,' said Mr Briggs as he welcomed Augusta and Philip into his plush Curzon Street office.

Philip was wearing his dull tweed suit and spectacles again and Augusta wore a jacket and skirt which she had bought for a special occasion before the war. The skirt's waistband was a little tight, but fortunately she wouldn't have to wear it for long.

'I hope you have some art to show us today, Mr Briggs,' she said.

'I do indeed!' He rubbed his plump hands together in expectation. 'Now, if you'd like to come with me, I have a car waiting for us.'

'A car?'

'Don't you like motor cars, Mrs Dennis?'

'Yes, but I thought you would have the artworks in your office here.' Augusta didn't like the thought of being taken somewhere. She could tell from Philip's expression that he felt anxious about it too.

'I don't keep works of art on these premises,' said Mr Briggs. 'I have them stored somewhere.'

'Very well.'

Augusta reassured herself that Detective Inspector Morris and his men were watching the building from a vehicle. Once they noticed Augusta and Philip being driven away, they would be sure to follow.

'Excellent. Let's go!'

Mr Briggs put on his hat, and they followed him out of his office. He led them along an unfamiliar corridor, then stepped through a door which led into a small courtyard. The buildings loomed tall over them and a narrow alleyway provided the only access to the street. A black Ford sedan car waited for them.

Augusta's stomach tightened. She didn't trust Briggs. But if she and Philip refused to go with him, he'd be suspicious.

'What a lovely motor car,' she said with forced cheeriness.

The driver got out to open the rear doors for them. He had broad shoulders, a thick neck and a pugnacious face.

Reluctantly, Augusta got into the car. Philip sat beside her and Briggs got into the front passenger seat.

'Right then!' He rubbed his palms together again. 'Let's be on our way.'

Their route zig-zagged through a maze of narrow streets before joining the wide thoroughfare of Piccadilly. Detective Inspector Morris and his men were watching the building from Curzon Street. Augusta could only hope they had chosen to watch the rear of the building too.

From Piccadilly Circus, they travelled along Regent Street and then into Trafalgar Square and eastwards into the Strand. Mr Briggs made conversation about the weather and Augusta attempted to cheerfully respond.

The expression on Philip's face was grim. She nudged his knee to remind him he was supposed to be in character.

They passed along Fleet Street and Ludgate Hill, towards the enormous dome of St Paul's Cathedral. Once they were beyond it, the car took them through the City and past the grand classical Bank of England and Royal Exchange. Augusta willed the car to slow and turn into a side street. But they continued on, turning north into Bishopsgate and towards Liverpool Street station. They were now on the boundary of the City of London and the east end. Commerce and wealth on Augusta's left, criminality and poverty on her right.

The car turned right into Brushfield Street, then right again into a little network of streets lined with tall narrow houses, pubs and scruffy shops. They were in a rundown area called Spitalfields. The car bounced on the uneven cobbles and a group of children stared at them as they passed.

'This is where you store your artworks?' Philip asked. 'It doesn't look like the safest street to me.'

'It's not the nicest area,' said Briggs. 'But that has its advantages. Nobody would ever believe that valuable paintings are being stored here under their noses.' He gave a chuckle.

The car stopped outside a house with shuttered windows. The driver opened the doors for them and they followed Briggs, who had a key for the shabby door.

'Follow me,' he said.

The house smelt damp and musty and didn't seem lived in. Briggs led them up a flight of narrow wooden stairs. Augusta prayed Detective Inspector Morris's men had followed them here. As soon as they set eyes on the stolen artworks, they needed to get outside again and raise the alarm.

Philip made slow progress up the stairs with his walking stick. Eventually he reached the little landing at the top and Briggs led them on to the next flight of stairs. 'Nearly there,' he said.

The stairwell was lit by a narrow window covered with dusty cobwebs. Augusta gave a shiver and willed herself on.

At the top of the house, Briggs showed them into a room with tall sash windows. The glass was filthy, and some of the panes were cracked and broken. An old loom took up half of the room. The timber structure was fixed to floor and ceiling. The frame was broken and sections of it lay at the foot of the wall. A spinning wheel sat beneath one of the windows.

'This is an old silk weaver's house, as you've probably guessed,' said Briggs.

'And the artworks?' asked Augusta.

'In the other room. I'll fetch them for you now.'

'Thank you.' Augusta let out a breath which she had been holding onto. Perhaps Briggs would be as good as his word after all.

He left the room and shut the door behind him. Then there was the unmistakable sound of a key turning in the lock.

'Has he locked us in?' said Philip. He walked over to the door and tried the handle. 'He has!' He hammered on the door. 'Briggs?'

There was no sound.

Augusta heard a car starting in the street. She dashed over to the window and rubbed some of the grime away with her sleeve. She was just in time to see the Ford sedan driving away.

'He's gone,' she said.

Chapter 30

'UNBELIEVABLE!' Philip rattled the door and pulled at the handle. 'He must have discovered who we are. We underestimated him, didn't we? How could he have worked it out?'

'Perhaps he did some research into us,' said Augusta. 'Perhaps he visited the address in West Norwood and realised Mr and Mrs Dennis didn't live there. I can't believe he would have gone to such lengths to do that, but he's selling stolen works of art. So he's going to do all he can to protect himself.'

Philip sighed. 'I think you could be right, Augusta. But why lock us in this place? What's he going to do with us? We have to get out of here.' He walked over to the window. 'And where on earth is Morris and his men?'

'If they managed to follow us here, then they may have followed Briggs when he departed,' said Augusta. 'And maybe they'll come back for us shortly.'

'I think that's looking on the bright side. Morris probably has no idea we're here at all. He was in a vehicle on Curzon Street waiting for me to emerge and take off my hat with my left hand. He's probably still there now, wondering what's keeping us! Briggs must have known the Curzon Street entrance would be watched. Or if he didn't know it, he made an educated guess. That's why we left the building via the courtyard.' He rubbed at the grimy window. 'Can we climb out of here?'

'No, we can't. We're on the second floor.'

'How many feet is that?'

'At least twenty. And probably more,' said Augusta. 'It's much too risky.'

Philip turned to her. 'Well, that all depends on what Briggs has got in store for us, doesn't it? If he's going to slowly torture us to death, then I'd much rather break both legs jumping out of a window.'

'Oh, don't!' Augusta felt cold inside.

'Hello!' shouted Philip. 'There's someone down there. Do you think he can hear us?' He pushed and pulled at the sash window. 'This frame won't budge. We could smash the windows.'

'And risk injuring the people on the street,' said Augusta. 'There were children playing out there earlier.'

'We could do it at night when they're not around.'

'Smash the windows and do what?'

'Shout out for help. Hopefully, someone will be willing to break the door down.'

Philip returned to the door and rattled it again. 'It opens inwards,' he said. 'That makes it difficult to break down from this side. If we could somehow kick the frame…'

'Do you want me to try?' said Augusta, knowing his injured leg would make it difficult for him to do it. She and Philip had successfully broken doors down in the past.

'Yes please, Augusta. See if you can break the frame.'

Augusta hoisted her skirt up a little, raised her leg and aimed a kick at the door frame. It splintered a little but didn't break. She tried again and pain shot up her leg. 'Ouch!'

'Are you alright?'

'Not really.'

After ten minutes of trying, Augusta was too tired to continue.

'You've caused quite a bit of damage,' said Philip, examining the splintered frame. 'Maybe you can have another go when you've recovered. Now what about these hinges? Perhaps we can loosen them. They look rather old and rusted up, though.'

Augusta sat down on the floor and rested against the timber loom frame. The waistband of her skirt was too tight. She unfastened the button at the back, but it made little difference.

'I must get into the habit of carrying skeleton keys with me,' said Philip, peering through the lock on the door. 'It would help in situations like this. Is there any wire in this room?' He began searching for some.

'I haven't seen any,' said Augusta. 'And I think Briggs will be back soon. He knows people will be looking for us. He can't keep us here for long.'

'I wish I could believe you, Augusta. But I think you're being over hopeful.'

'Maybe Morris knows Briggs uses this place?' she continued. 'Perhaps he'll be here shortly?'

'I like to think so, but I don't know.' Philip continued looking around the room. 'I'm wondering if Morris has been mistaken. Maybe Briggs doesn't have any paintings at all.'

'He had better do,' said Augusta. 'I don't wish to be locked up here for nothing!'

'I can't find any wire,' said Philip. 'Briggs had better come back soon. As soon as we hear his footsteps on the staircase, we get ready to rush at him as soon as he comes in through the door. He can't detain us here.' He walked over to the broken pieces of the loom and picked up a yard-long section of the frame. 'I can whack him over the head with this.'

'But what if he's accompanied by someone else?'

'We just rush them. The element of surprise will catch them off guard and we make our escape.'

'And if they have a weapon?'

'We'll obviously have to be careful. If we can't physically take them on, then we can at least make as much noise as possible. Someone out on the street is bound to hear.'

Chapter 31

'I'm sorry I'm late, Miss Kingsley,' said Cedric Langley as he stepped into her apartment. He wore a mint green jacket with matching trousers and a gold waistcoat.

'You're not sorry. You're always late.'

'Not always.' He placed a hand on his chest, as if offended by her words. He went to sit down in the chair across the fireplace from her.

'No need to sit, Cedric. This won't take long.'

'Won't take long?' He straightened up again and puffed out his chest. 'But I was going to ask how you are, Miss Kingsley.'

'How do you think I am?'

'I'd say you were shocked and saddened.'

'Correct. So there was no need to ask me, was there?'

'I suppose not.' He gave a bemused smile. 'Cigarette?'

'No, thank you.'

'Have the police worked out what happened to Lola yet?'

'Not yet. Have they spoken to you?'

'Yes. And I've told them what I know.'

'Me too.'

'Someone must have got into the changing rooms.'

'I think that's obvious.'

'Did you not see her in there?'

'No, I didn't!' She felt her teeth clench. 'Why does everyone ask me that?'

'I suppose it's surprising you didn't notice her.'

'If I had seen her then I would have…' She checked herself. 'Well, it's obvious I would have been angry.'

He gave her a curious glance, and she didn't like it.

'I'm very disappointed about the photographs, Cedric.'

'Me too! From now on, I will always have a second camera with me.'

'That doesn't help us now, does it?'

'No.'

'And the photographs which you did manage to take were awful.'

'I'm sorry?'

'The clothes look awful in them.'

He gave a sniff. 'It seems the entire afternoon needs to be forgotten about, then.'

'If only we could do that!' She got to her feet. 'The entire thing has been a complete disaster.'

'It has.' Cedric shrank back a little. 'They'll catch him before long.'

'They had better do. Who do you think did it, Cedric?'

'Who do I think? Well, I really don't know. I mean… it could have been one of the other girls, but I really can't believe any of them would have done such a thing. So someone else must have got in there. But who and why, I really don't know. And how would they have got in and out of the changing rooms without being seen?'

'Exactly. That's what puzzles me, too.' She sank back

into her chair again. 'Detective Sergeant Joyce visited me this afternoon.'

'And what was he asking?'

'He asked me if Lola had known about the stolen money.'

'What stolen money?'

'That's what I asked him. He was assuming I already knew about it. And I knew nothing of it. But you know all about it, don't you, Cedric?'

His lips moved as he thought about his reply. 'What are you specifically referring to, Miss Kingsley?'

'The charity fashion show we held in May.'

'Oh, that.'

'No one told me some money went missing from the amount we had raised. The children's charity didn't receive all of it.'

'Didn't they?'

'Stop acting like you know nothing about it, Cedric! That Scotland Yard detective told me everything. You took twenty-five pounds, didn't you?'

His face paled. He staggered over to the chair and sank into it. 'Yes,' he said quietly. 'I did take it. But I paid it back and apologised. I sorted it all out with Miss Bilston and she promised not to say anything more about it.'

'But she got the police involved.'

'Yes, she did. And that was before I spoke to her about it. She didn't realise I'd taken it, you see. But I explained the situation to everyone, and the charity got all their money in the end, and I feel terribly ashamed about the whole affair.'

'Did Lola know you took the money?'

'No! Only Miss Bilston and the police. It was nothing, really. More a misunderstanding than anything.'

'We raised over a hundred pounds for the children's charity that day and you helped yourself to a quarter of it.'

'I borrowed it. I regret it very deeply.'

'You stole it and only repaid the money when you were found out.'

'It was always my intention to repay it.'

'What did you even need twenty-five pounds for? People only need to look at your home and clothes to see you're not short of money.'

He pursed his lips. 'I had to pay for something and there was no other option available to me at the time.'

Vivien shook her head. 'I used to have high opinions of you, Cedric.'

He sat back and crossed his legs. 'I apologise for not being perfect.' He inhaled on his cigarette. 'Why did the detective want to know if Lola knew about the money?'

'He wanted to know if she'd been silenced.'

'By whom? Me?'

'I think that's what the detective was suggesting.'

'Well, he's wrong!'

'Tell him that, then.'

'I will if he speaks to me again. But I'm not deliberately seeking him out.'

Vivien decided to bring the conversation to a close. She checked the gold watch on her wrist. 'I need to get on,' she said, getting to her feet.

'Of course.' Cedric stubbed out his cigarette and stood up. 'I'm sorry our conversation wasn't happier.'

'So am I. Thank you for your work over the years, Cedric, but I'm letting you go.'

His lips thinned, and he looked down at the floor, then up at the ceiling. Then he blinked a few times and left the apartment without a further word.

Chapter 32

'This reminds me of the time we were shut in that cupboard in Belgium, Augusta,' said Philip. 'At least this room is a little larger.'

'That was when we were working in that restaurant in Ghent and the German officers locked us up while they checked our identity papers,' said Augusta. 'I really thought we were for it then.'

'Fortunately for us, British intelligence was exceptionally good at forgeries. But we did well to get out of there that evening. Clearly we'd raised the German officers' suspicions.'

Almost two hours had passed since Briggs had left them. It was almost five o'clock now. Philip and Augusta had made two more attempts to break the door frame, but they had failed.

Augusta gave a sigh. 'I have to remind myself this isn't as dangerous as it was during the war.'

'Well, you say that, but we don't know for sure, do we?' Philip got to his feet and stretched his legs. 'We don't know what Briggs is capable of.'

'He would be stupid to harm us.'

'Yes, he would. But it all depends on how keen he is to protect his stolen treasures. If Morris has no idea where we are and Briggs returns in the dead of night and murders us... our bodies could be dumped in a ditch in Kent by first light tomorrow.'

'Oh, good grief Philip! You really know how to keep our spirits up, don't you?' Augusta got to her feet and brushed off her skirt. It slipped a little from where she had loosened the zip. Now she was standing, she had to tighten it again. She had a stomach ache. She couldn't work out if it was from the tight waistband or the worry about their situation.

She walked over to the windows and tried to open them.

'They're stuck fast,' said Philip.

'Yes, I realise that. I just hoped that...'

'You could somehow open them? Even after I've already spent ages trying.'

'Yes, it's irrational. I realise that. But we have to do something, don't we? We can't just wait for Briggs to return with his murder squad.'

'He might not be planning to kill us.'

'You say that now. But a moment ago, you seemed quite sure of it!'

'I was never sure of it, it was just a worry... oh, Augusta, let's not argue. The stress is getting to both of us, and we need to stay friends to cope with this.'

'You're right.' Much as she willed them away, tears sprung into her eyes. She turned back to the window and dabbed at her eyes with the sleeve of her jacket.

She heard Philip's steps behind her. Then she felt his hand on her shoulder. 'Come on,' he said softly.

She turned to him and they embraced. She hid her

face against his shoulder, feeling embarrassed about her tears. The tweed of his jacket felt rough on her skin.

'Sorry,' she said.

'For what?'

'For getting upset. For getting angry.'

'There's no need to apologise. It's normal to feel that way when you've been locked up by a criminal who looks like a beetroot.'

Augusta giggled. 'A beetroot?'

'It's that red face of his. And he's quite round, too.' He released her from the embrace and gently moved her hair from her face. Their eyes met now, just inches apart. 'I'm sorry for being snappy and talking about murder,' he said. 'It was unreasonable of me.'

His eyes held hers, and she wondered if he was about to kiss her. And if he wasn't, should she kiss him?

The sound of an engine broke the silence. A vehicle had pulled up outside the building.

'That could be...'

'Yes.'

Augusta didn't want to pull away from Philip, but Briggs now occupied her mind again. She stepped over to the window and looked through the bit they had wiped clean.

The Ford sedan was back.

'He's here,' she said.

Philip picked up the piece of wood from the loom frame and went over to the door.

Augusta could hear footsteps on the ground floor. She held her breath as they climbed the stairs.

Philip stood poised near the door. His weapon in his hand.

'I don't think you should attack him,' she whispered. 'It might make matters worse.'

'We have to get out of here,' he said. 'Alive.'

Augusta's heart pounded as the steps grew nearer. Then she heard the floorboards creak on the other side of the door.

'It's Briggs,' said a voice. 'Don't try anything funny when I come in there. I've got two men with me. I advise you to stand back from the door.'

'We should do what he says,' Augusta whispered to Philip.

Philip laid down the piece of wood and moved away from the door. 'Alright Briggs,' he said. 'In you come.'

The key turned in the lock and Briggs stepped into the room. Two large men stood behind him. Augusta recognised one of them as the well-built driver.

'Good evening.' Briggs grinned as he stepped into the room. His men remained by the door. 'I'm sorry to keep you cooped up like this, Mr and Mrs Dennis. But I'm sure you understand my reasons.'

'This is how you treat all your clients, is it?' said Philip.

'Only the ones who lie to me.'

'Who's lying to you?'

'You are, Mr Philip Fisher. Formerly a detective inspector at Scotland Yard. And Mrs Augusta Peel.' He turned to her with a smile. 'A bookseller who fancies herself as a private detective. Not very good at it, are you? I got an odd feeling from the pair of you when you turned up at my office last week. I got a man to watch you. You seem to think I'm easily fooled.'

'How about you let us go, Briggs?' said Philip. 'Scotland Yard know we met with you this afternoon. They'll be searching for us.'

'Yes, I'm sure they will be. But they won't think of looking here, will they?'

'What are you hoping to achieve?' asked Augusta.

'I'm teaching you a lesson,' said Mr Briggs. 'You seem to think you can wander into my office and somehow get your hands on some art by pretending to be Mr and Mrs Dennis of West Norwood. It's all quite amusing and desperately amateurish.'

'The art is stolen,' said Philip. 'Where is it?'

Briggs laughed. 'You expect me to tell you, Fisher? And the art is not stolen. Each piece has been acquired legally.'

'You don't acquire art legally, Briggs. Or should I call you Fleming? You probably have other aliases too. The Yard is on to you. Your days are numbered.'

Augusta clenched her teeth. She felt anxious about Philip antagonising Briggs. There was a chance he might harm them.

'The Yard can't prove anything,' said Briggs.

'If you're not worried about them, then why did you lock us up here?'

'Because you're a nuisance, Fisher. And so are you, Mrs Peel. I could have met with a client who actually wanted to buy from me rather than waste my time with you two.'

'The longer you keep us here, the more trouble you're going to be in when the Yard catches you.'

'If the Yard catches me. But as I say, they can't prove anything.'

'Keeping us detained here is illegal,' said Philip. 'They'll have you for that.'

'Well, that depends on you, doesn't it, Mr Fisher?'

'And what do you mean by that?'

Briggs pulled a piece of paper out of his jacket pocket. He proceeded to read out an address in Bognor Regis.

Augusta felt her heart sink. Philip's estranged wife and his young son lived in Bognor Regis.

'Who lives there?' said Philip as nonchalantly as possible.

'You can pretend you're not familiar with that address if you like, Fisher. But both you and I know it's where your family live.'

'Not anymore,' said Philip. 'They've moved.'

'They moved? And when was that? Five minutes ago? I know they were at that address yesterday. Your wife was wearing a pretty pink summer dress when she took your son for a walk with her mother. They've had some nice weather down there these past few days.'

Philip's face paled. 'If you lay one finger on my family, Briggs, you'll swing for it. I swear!'

Chapter 33

Augusta and Philip left the house in Spitalfields and found their way through the narrow streets to busy Commercial Street. They hailed a taxi. 'Scotland Yard,' Philip said to the taxi driver. 'As fast as possible, please.'

The relief at their safe release was marred by the threat to Philip's family. 'What a disaster,' he said. 'Briggs saw right through us and now my family is in danger. They're going to have to move. And it's going to be a huge inconvenience for them. I wish I'd never got involved in this case.'

'We underestimated Briggs,' said Augusta.

'Yes, we did. And Morris underestimated him, too. Briggs has been a criminal for decades. He's wise to every trick in the book.'

The taxi stopped by the tall gates of Scotland Yard on the riverside at Westminster. Philip paid the driver and walked as briskly as he could into the building.

'I need someone to liaise with the police in Bognor,' he said to Augusta. 'My family needs protecting.'

The sergeant behind the desk recognised him. 'Good evening, sir. It's good to see you again. How can I help?'

'Is Detective Inspector Morris in?'

'Yes, I saw him come in a short while ago.'

'It's reassuring to know he's looking for us.'

'I'm sorry?'

'Never mind. I'll go and see him.'

They found Detective Inspector Morris upstairs in his wood-panelled office with three other detectives.

'Fisher! What happened?'

'Briggs found us out. That's what happened. And he locked us in an old weaver's house in Spitalfields.'

'What? Why?'

'To teach us a lesson, he said. He'd told us he was taking us to see the artworks. I shouldn't have agreed to it. It was a stupid mistake.'

'But I don't understand,' said Detective Inspector Morris. 'We didn't see you leave the building on Curzon Street.'

'That's because Briggs took us out via an exit at the rear.'

'I didn't even know there was an exit at the rear.' Detective Inspector Morris turned to the other detectives. 'Did anyone else know there was a door at the rear?' They shook their heads.

Philip sighed. 'Proper surveillance should have been carried out.'

'Yes, I realise that now. We watched the building for a few hours, then Detective Sergeant Gallagher went in to ask for Mr Briggs and was told he was out. We were very confused because we hadn't seen him or you leave.'

'None of that matters now, anyway. Briggs locked us up, then returned with two large friends. He's threatened my family in Bognor Regis. He knows where they live.'

'Oh no.'

'He's clearly got someone down there watching them.

He saw my wife and my son yesterday.' Philip's voice cracked and there was a pause as he recovered himself.

Augusta felt tears at the back of her eyes. It was unusual for Philip to show emotion like this.

'Alright, Fisher. We'll make sure your family is looked after. I'll speak to the superintendent in Bognor Regis. We can't have your family being pulled into this.' He rubbed at his face. 'I regret asking you to help us, Fisher. We'll get over to Curzon Street again and arrest Briggs.'

'No. Not yet. We need him to lead us to the stolen artworks first. Lord Montpelier needs his painting back. As long as my family has protection, I'm willing to help. Just let me know how you get on with the superintendent at Bognor.'

'Oh, he'll help alright. I'll make sure of it. You have my word, Fisher.'

On their way out, they met Detective Sergeant Joyce. 'Fancy meeting the pair of you here! You'll be interested in a development in the Lola Parker case. I met with Miss Kingsley today to discuss Cedric Langley, the photographer, with her.'

'Why was that?'

'Sergeant Collins at Kensington T Division brought something to my attention. Apparently, he spoke to Mr Langley a few months ago about some charity money which was stolen. Miss Kingsley held a fashion show to raise funds for a children's charity and some went missing. Twenty-five pounds, to be exact.'

'A month's salary for some people,' said Philip. 'Mr Langley stole the money?'

'Yes. And once he was found out, he paid it back rather quickly.'

'Did he explain why he'd taken it?'

'No, he wouldn't tell Sergeant Collins why he'd taken

it. I asked Miss Kingsley about it and she was unaware it had happened. It turns out her assistant, Miss Bilston, agreed to keep it from her.'

'So Langley persuaded Miss Bilston to keep it quiet from Miss Kingsley,' said Philip. 'I can't imagine she was happy about it when she found out.'

'No, she wasn't.'

'What could he have needed the money for?' asked Augusta.

'Sergeant Collins had a theory,' said Detective Sergeant Joyce. 'While he was looking into the case, he heard a rumour that Mr Langley had an affair with the son of a duke.'

'Which duke?' asked Philip.

'Collins didn't know. And he didn't know whether there was truth to it or just a rumour. However, if it was true and someone unscrupulous found out about it…'

'Blackmail,' said Philip.

Detective Sergeant Joyce nodded. 'Exactly.'

'Someone discovers a man is a homosexual and they want to make money out of it.'

'It's just a theory,' said Detective Sergeant Joyce. 'And Mr Langley repaid the money to the charity and the case against him was dropped. But he never explained what he needed the money for. Collins told me he didn't appear to have any vices such as gambling. He's a bachelor and has no family to support.'

'So the fact he was being blackmailed is just an assumption,' said Augusta.

'But a fair one I think,' said Philip. 'His refusal to explain what he needed the money for could hint at it. And the fact he needed a sum of money quickly and secretly suggests he was trying to silence someone.'

'If Cedric Langley was being blackmailed, then he

must have been running out of money,' said Augusta. 'Stealing from a children's charity is an act of desperation. And after being caught stealing, he couldn't really get away with it again, could he? So if he no longer had any money for his blackmailer… there was only one other solution.'

'Murder,' said Detective Sergeant Joyce.

'This could explain why Lola's flatmate told me she had lots of money to spend,' said Augusta. 'She could have been blackmailing Cedric Langley.'

'I'm going to speak to Cedric Langley tomorrow morning and put this to him,' said Detective Sergeant Joyce. 'You've both been very helpful. Can I call on you to accompany me tomorrow?'

'Of course,' said Augusta. 'We're happy to help.'

Chapter 34

CEDRIC LANGLEY'S flat was in Cornwall Mansions in Kensington: a row of grand Victorian buildings with columned porches and balconies. Philip was leaning against the railings when she arrived.

'Morning, Augusta. Have you recovered from yesterday's ordeal?'

'I think so. Have you spoken to your family?'

'Yes, I telephoned my wife late last night. Morris was true to his word and got the superintendent down there to look after them. They've got a constable at the door day and night at the moment.'

'Oh dear, that's not very nice for them. Is your wife annoyed about it?'

'Surprisingly not. In fact, she's quite concerned about me, which was nice. I hadn't expected her to still care.'

'Of course she does,' said Augusta, trying to ignore a pang of jealousy. 'You're her husband.'

'Estranged husband.'

'Well, as long as they're safe, that's all that matters.'

A police car pulled up in front of them and parked

behind an open top green Vauxhall car. Detective Sergeant Joyce gave them a wave as he climbed out.

'I'm worried Cedric Langley's going to feel outnumbered by us,' said Philip. 'Three of us and one of him.'

'He doesn't strike me as the sort to be intimidated,' said Augusta.

'Good morning!' said Joyce, joining them by the railings. His greeting was drowned out by the barking of three small terriers which were pulling a lady along the path towards them.

Two men stepped out of the apartment block. Augusta immediately recognised one of them as Cedric Langley. His companion headed for the car while Langley stared at Augusta for a moment.

'Mr Langley.' She took a step towards him. He looked at Philip, then Joyce, and skipped around the car to get into the passenger seat.

'Oi! Langley! I want a word with you!' shouted Joyce. He spoke just as the lady with the terriers was passing. The loudness of his voice sent the dogs into a frenzy. They lunged at his legs.

Joyce cried out in pain.

'Stop!' cried out the woman.

Langley's companion cranked the Vauxhall.

'Stop!' Philip shouted at him as he headed for the driver's door. 'Police!'

'Police? Where?' said the lady, trying to pull her dogs off Joyce. Joyce kicked at the dogs, but they clung onto him. Augusta pulled at their collars and managed to tug two of them away from Joyce's legs. They had made a hole in his trousers.

The Vauxhall moved off.

'Langley's getting away!' shouted Joyce. 'He knows we're onto him!'

'The man's clearly guilty,' said Philip. 'We've got to get after him!'

The woman pulled the third dog off Joyce. He slumped down against the railings and groaned as he clasped his shins.

'Oh, good grief!' said the lady. 'I'm so sorry!'

Joyce rolled up his trouser leg to reveal a trickle of blood. The lady shrieked and berated her dogs.

'Get Langley,' Joyce said.

'We can't leave you here,' said Philip.

'Yes, you can. I'll be fine. But get Langley. Only a guilty man would take off like that.' He held out the key for the car.

Augusta and Philip exchanged a glance.

'You'll have to drive, Augusta,' said Philip. 'You know I'm unable to with my leg.'

'Of course.' She turned to Joyce. 'Are you sure you'll be all right?'

'Yes, I'll be fine. I'll make sure I see a doctor. Don't let Langley get away.'

'I'll look after him,' said the lady with the dogs. 'I'm so sorry about what happened. I feel so awful about it.'

'There's no time to waste,' said Philip. He cranked the car while Augusta got into the driver's seat.

As soon as Philip was in the car beside her, she went after the Vauxhall.

Chapter 35

AUGUSTA ACCELERATED the car as fast as she could to the end of the road where she had to stop at a junction.

'There they are!' said Philip, pointing to the right.

She pushed the car out into the traffic, apologising to the driver she had forced to stop, and turned into Gloucester Road. The green Vauxhall was held up in the traffic ahead of them. It swerved around an omnibus and turned left at the bottom of Gloucester Road into Cromwell Road.

Augusta and Philip followed.

'He didn't even hang about to talk to us, did he?' shouted Philip over the noise of the engine. 'He must be guilty of something.'

She negotiated the slow-moving traffic, edging around a van. She tried to keep the Vauxhall in their sight as she drove. They passed the grand edifice of the Natural History Museum and then the Victoria and Albert Museum.

'Where can they possibly be heading?' she said.

'We'll find out,' said Philip. 'I wonder if this is the trip they had planned or whether it's just an attempt to evade us.'

Cromwell Road had now become Brompton Road, and they followed the Vauxhall as best they could. As they entered Knightsbridge, Augusta got stuck behind a slow-moving truck. She tried to find an opportunity to get around it, aware that the Vauxhall was speeding on ahead.

'There's enough space for you to get around!' shouted Philip.

'No, I don't think there is.'

'Yes, there is! Just nudge out. The cars coming the other way will have to slow down for you.'

Augusta clenched her teeth and manoeuvred into the oncoming traffic. A car coming the other way beeped its horn. She gave an apologetic wave and sped up.

The green Vauxhall took a sudden turn to the right and swung across oncoming traffic by Hyde Park Corner.

'Good grief!' said Philip.

Augusta followed, swerving the car to the right and hoping everything else would get out of her way. She could feel her heart pounding as they followed the Vauxhall past the grand Wellington Arch and along Constitution Hill. Parkland extended either side of the road, Green Park to the left and the gardens of Buckingham Palace to the right.

'Perhaps Cedric Langley has an urgent appointment with the King,' said Philip.

They followed the Vauxhall around the bend at the end of Constitution Hill and to the front of Buckingham Palace. The car then took a sharp turn left and sped off along The Mall.

'No, I don't think he wants to see the King,' said Augusta.

She accelerated along The Mall, passing St James's Palace on the left and St James's Park on the right.

'Excellent work, Augusta, you're gaining on them!'

Sure enough, they were getting closer to the Vauxhall ahead of them.

'Let's hope they're low on petrol,' said Augusta.

'If they run out, we've got them,' said Philip. 'Although I don't know how much petrol we've got in this car.'

Ahead of them was the end of The Mall and Admiralty Arch. They followed the Vauxhall beneath the arch and then left and around Trafalgar Square.

'Well, we're certainly getting a tour of the sights,' said Philip, pointing out Nelson's Column.

They followed the Vauxhall past the columned facade of the National Gallery and turned off to the left, heading up Charing Cross Road. The traffic was slow, but the Vauxhall was just ahead of them.

'Beep the horn at them, Augusta!'

She did so and Philip leant out of the window. 'Stop!' he shouted, 'pull over!'

Without warning, the Vauxhall took a sharp left down Cranbourn Street. Pedestrians had to skip out of the way. Philip was flung against Augusta as she made the turn.

'Good reactions, Augusta. He's trying desperately to lose us, isn't he?'

They followed the Vauxhall through Leicester Square, past the Empire Theatre, and on into Coventry Street and towards Piccadilly Circus.

'Now we're going back on ourselves,' she said. 'I don't think they have an idea about where to go. They're panicking.'

At Piccadilly Circus, the Vauxhall passed the Shaftesbury Memorial and swung into Regent Street. The wide thoroughfare gave the car plenty of space to pass around the slower vehicles. Augusta followed close behind. Then the Vauxhall made a sudden left turn into Conduit Street.

'This is going to go on until someone runs out of petrol, isn't it?' said Philip. They followed the car right into New Bond Street.

'I don't understand what Cedric is hoping to achieve,' said Augusta. 'Whatever happens, we'll catch up with him at some point.'

They turned left onto Brook Street and headed on into Grosvenor Square. The Vauxhall circled the entire circumference of Grosvenor Square before heading into a narrow street at the bottom corner. Augusta followed, but a car got in her way. She beeped at it to move, and the driver made a rude gesture.

They turned right just in time to see the Vauxhall turning left. But when Augusta turned left, they couldn't see the Vauxhall anymore.

'Bother!' said Philip.

Augusta slowed the car and stopped opposite a right-hand turning. 'They could have gone down there,' she said.

'Possibly. I think we should go on.'

A crossroads lay ahead. Augusta stopped the car to check each direction, but there was no sign of the Vauxhall.

She sighed. 'I think we've lost them.'

'Let's just drive around here a little bit and see if we can find them,' said Philip.

They spent the next few minutes driving around the crisscrossing streets of Mayfair. Past grand townhouses, upmarket restaurants and gentlemen's clubs. They eventually emerged on Piccadilly. Augusta headed west on Piccadilly, then turned right into Park Lane.

'They must have gone down that little lane I pointed out,' she said. 'If they went down there, then they would have found their way into Hyde Park. If they sped through Hyde Park, then they could be anywhere by now.'

'What a nuisance,' said Philip. 'But we'll catch up with Cedric and his friend. Let's get over to the Yard and make sure all divisions are on the lookout for the green Vauxhall. Cedric Langley won't get away with this.'

Chapter 36

Augusta couldn't decide if it was tea or coffee which had been spilt over *The Mayor of Casterbridge* by Thomas Hardy. Whichever it was, it had left a large stain on the plum-coloured cover. She dipped a cloth into a bowl of soapy water, then gently wiped at the stain, hoping she could remove the worst of it.

Had Lola Parker been blackmailing Cedric Langley? Augusta felt frustrated the photographer had got away before they could ask him. He clearly had something to hide. And who was his companion?

Mr Langley had to be the main suspect now. He had already admitted he had gone into the changing rooms that afternoon to take photographs. He could have gone into the changing rooms a second time without raising much suspicion. And had he known Lola was in there alone? Augusta felt sure he would have realised it during the final part of the show when she didn't appear on stage. And if he had gone into the changing rooms at that time, then it explained why he had taken no photographs of the final part. He claimed his camera had broken, but it was possible he was lying.

Augusta felt sure Detective Sergeant Joyce would arrest him as soon as he got the chance. She could only hope Mr Langley hadn't fled London altogether.

A raised voice from beyond the door startled her. She stopped her work and stepped out into the shop to find Fred standing behind the counter. A lanky young man stood on the other side, pointing a finger at him.

It was Eddie Miller.

'You stay away from Harriet, do you hear?'

'I have never intentionally gone near her,' said Fred. 'She's a regular customer in this shop and I have merely helped her choose books to read. There is nothing more to it than that.'

'I know what you're planning!'

'I'm not planning anything,' said Fred, holding his hands up.

Augusta could tell from the shakiness in his voice that he was frightened.

She stepped forward. 'I know who you are, Eddie,' she said. 'And you can't walk into my shop and speak to my staff like that. I'm asking you to leave.'

He stared at her for a moment. 'You're the lady who came to the factory. What are you doing here?'

'This is my shop.'

'Is it? Well, I've come to have a word with him.' He jabbed his finger at Fred again.

'Leave now before I call the police,' said Augusta.

'The police won't be interested,' said Eddie.

'Yes, they will,' said Augusta. 'Now leave.'

Eddie took a few steps back. 'Fine, I'll leave. But only if your friend here agrees to fight me outside. Like a proper man.'

'He won't be doing anything of the sort!' said Augusta. 'Get out!'

'He knows I'll beat him,' said Eddie. He fixed Fred with a taunting stare. 'I'll beat him to a pulp. He's got no chance against someone like me. Look at him, he's scared.'

'Scared, am I?' In a swift movement, Fred stepped out from behind the counter and strode towards the young man.

'Looks like we're on!' said Eddie with a laugh of delight.

'Fred!' called out Augusta. 'Don't get involved. Ignore him!'

But Fred was too consumed with anger to listen. The two men left the shop and Augusta followed.

Out on the street, Eddie pulled off his jacket, flung it to the ground and rolled up his shirt sleeves. 'Fancy a fight then, do you, Fred? Trying to prove yourself to Harriet, are you? You're going to be very ashamed when I beat you.'

Fred stepped forward. 'Go away,' he said. 'And stay away.'

Eddie gave him a shove and Fred took a stumble back.

'Stop it!' said Augusta. She didn't know whether to go back into the shop to telephone the police or remain outside to prevent a serious fight from happening. 'The pair of you! Please stop it!'

Eddie pushed Fred again and this time Fred gave him a strong shove which sent him tumbling backwards. He fell to the ground, but quickly jumped to his feet again.

Augusta despaired. Neither of them was listening to her. She glanced quickly around, looking for anyone who could help. Passers-by crossed the road to avoid getting involved.

The two young men held their fists up now, sparring with each other. Eddie threw a punch, but Fred ducked.

Then Eddie lashed out again and Fred grabbed hold of his arm. A scuffle began as they pushed each other back and forth and traded blows.

Augusta took a step back. There was nothing she could do to break it up without getting hurt herself. Why had Fred allowed himself to get drawn into it?

'Someone call the police!' she shouted out. 'Is there a constable nearby?'

The shop door opened and Philip stepped out. 'What on earth is going on here?'

'Eddie Miller has provoked Fred,' she said. 'I can't break it up.'

Philip stepped over to the pair. 'Knock it off!' he shouted. 'Now!' He raised his walking stick and rapped it on Eddie's shins. The young man gave a howl of pain. Philip then seized Fred's arm and pulled him back. 'Break it up, the pair of you!' he hollered.

The two young men stood panting and glaring at each other. Philip stepped between them and Eddie wiped a trickle of blood from his nose.

'Eddie Miller,' said Philip. 'I've heard a lot about you.'

'Is that right? And who are you?'

'Mr Fisher, formerly a detective inspector of Scotland Yard. Now you get out of here quickly before I call my colleagues.'

Eddie sneered and picked up his jacket. He flung it over his shoulder, turned his back on them and sauntered off.

Fred put his face in his hands. 'I'm so sorry,' he said. 'I shouldn't have let myself get angry like that.' Augusta patted his shoulder. 'I couldn't help myself,' he continued. 'When he taunted me like that, I just wanted to silence him.'

'I'm not surprised,' said Philip. 'It takes a lot of discipline to resist a chap taunting you like that. But fellows like that Eddie Miller aren't quite right in the head. Getting involved with them is never worth it.'

Chapter 37

'I'll make sure Eddie's arrested for assaulting you, Fred,' said Philip once they were back inside the shop.

'No, there's no need. I'm not hurt, and I was just as much to blame. I shouldn't have agreed to fight him,' said Fred. 'And besides, I don't want Harriet to be drawn into this.'

'Has Harriet ever mentioned Eddie?' asked Augusta.

'No, never. I don't understand why a girl as lovely as her has anything to do with him.'

'Perhaps she doesn't. Not intentionally, anyway. Eddie Miller can be a bit of a nuisance, from what I've heard.'

'What do you know about him?'

'Lola Parker was his girlfriend,' said Augusta. 'And he struggled to accept their relationship was over.'

'So maybe something similar happened with Harriet?'

'Perhaps.'

'I'm going to make sure the police keep an eye on him,' said Philip. 'I respect your wishes, Fred, so I won't ask them to arrest him for attacking you. But if there's something else they can collar him for, then they can hopefully keep him off the streets.'

Fred sighed and leant against the counter.

'Are you alright, Fred?' Augusta asked.

'I'm fine. Just a little shaken up.'

'Why don't you go up to my office and have a rest in one of the easy chairs?' said Philip. 'There's a cup of tea up there too which I haven't started yet. I was interrupted by the fracas outside. You can help yourself to it.'

Fred thanked him and went upstairs.

'Poor Fred,' said Augusta, as she fed some bird seed to Sparky. 'Eddie Miller is clearly a nasty piece of work.'

'It makes you wonder what he's capable of,' said Philip. 'Joyce hasn't yet found anyone who saw him inside Holland Park Rink. But if he can find a witness, then I feel sure Eddie was capable of attacking Miss Parker.'

'But what about Cedric Langley?'

'Ah, yes. There's him as well.'

'We need to find out if Lola was blackmailing him. I'd like to visit her flatmate, Miss Roberts, again and ask her some more questions.'

'That's an excellent idea.' Philip checked his watch. 'If you leave now, you'll be there in time for when she finishes work.'

'Fred's resting and I can't leave the shop.'

'I'll mind the shop.'

Augusta laughed. 'Really?'

'Don't look so surprised! I used to help Mrs Charlton in her corner shop at the end of my street when I was a boy.'

'That was…'

'Some time ago? I know what you're suggesting, Augusta. But I won't hear it. I'm more than capable of looking after your shop. Now run along.'

'You'll need to look after Sparky too.'
'I'll manage. Off you go.'

Chapter 38

Augusta made the twenty-minute walk to the Bourne Estate in nearby Holborn.

'Oh, hello again, Mrs Peel,' said Mabel Roberts. She looked tired from her day of work. 'Have the police made any progress, do you know?'

'A little,' said Augusta.

'That's something, I suppose. It would be good if they could catch him, though. He might do it to someone else.'

'Hopefully not. But I suppose there's a risk until they're caught.' Augusta made herself comfortable on the little sofa in the sitting room. 'This is a delicate question to ask, Miss Roberts, but it's something I've been wondering. Do you know if Lola was blackmailing anyone?'

Mabel gasped. 'Blackmail? No, she would never have done such a thing.'

'You mentioned Lola had money to spend and I'm wondering where she could have got it from. I've heard Miss Kingsley only pays her models five pounds a week.'

'Is that all? Then Lola must have got the money from the secret boyfriend. Maybe he was rich.'

'You mentioned Lola came from an ordinary background,' said Augusta, 'unlike the other models who work for Miss Kingsley. Perhaps Lola felt she needed money so she could afford a similar lifestyle to them?'

'Yes, she probably thought that.'

'And blackmail is a way of making money.'

'She wouldn't have done that!' Mabel scowled, and it was the first time Augusta had seen her annoyed. She decided not to mention blackmail again. 'It would be useful to find out the secret boyfriend's identity,' she said. 'Do you mind if I have a look in Lola's bedroom? I know the police have searched it, but there may be a clue which they didn't spot.'

'Yes, alright then.' Mabel took Augusta to Lola's room, which was next to the sitting room. 'It's just as she left it,' she said, her voice cracking a little. 'Well, almost as she left it. The police didn't put everything back properly. So I did that so it's just how she would have wanted it.'

'I promise not to disturb anything,' said Augusta.

'I'll make some tea.' Mabel went off to the little kitchenette. Augusta sensed she was still annoyed with her for suggesting Lola could have blackmailed someone.

A stale perfume smell lingered in the small bedroom. A rose pink eiderdown covered the bed, and the dressing table was crowded with pots of makeup, bottles of perfume and trinkets. Necklaces were draped over the rectangular mirror which stood on the dressing table. Most of them looked cheap, but a few caught Augusta's eye. One had a small enamel jewelled egg as a pendant.

Augusta pictured Lola sitting on the little cushioned stool at her dressing table, applying her makeup and brushing her hair, trying to look her best. It was desperately sad she would never return to this room.

On the bedside table stood a fringed lamp, pots of face

cream, a handheld mirror, a silk sleep mask and a jewellery box. Augusta lifted the lid of the jewellery box and found it filled with earrings, rings and bracelets. There were one or two expensive items such as a ring which had an emerald encircled by diamonds. A gift from the secret boyfriend? Or bought with money Lola had acquired from blackmail?

In the chest of drawers, everything was overfilled and disorganised. Stockings had been crammed in with chemises, corsets and a variety of other undergarments. Thick winter clothing had been forced into the drawers at the bottom which couldn't close properly.

The wardrobe was filled with dresses, blouses, skirts, and trousers. The floor of the wardrobe was covered with shoes and handbags. More shoes were stacked along the skirting board. Some had acquired a thin layer of dust.

Where had Lola kept her personal papers? Had she kept a diary? It was possible the police had taken them away, but Detective Sergeant Joyce hadn't mentioned them.

Lola had been secretive. But how secretive? Augusta searched the drawers again but found no diary or letters.

She stood back and surveyed the room. If she had been Lola, where would she have hidden things she didn't want people to find?

Augusta had a thought. She stepped over to the bed, lifted one side of the eiderdown, then lifted the mattress. On top of the bed frame slats lay a large, battered envelope.

Augusta smiled. Why hadn't the police looked here?

She picked up the envelope, then lowered the mattress. Sitting on the bed, she pulled out the papers from the envelope. There were a few letters from a friend called Joanne in Manchester and another letter from an aunt in Norfolk.

The letters were chatty and informal but didn't shed any light on anything new.

There was a pocket-sized diary alongside the letters. Augusta opened it. A week was displayed across two pages so there wasn't much space to write. Every page until the date of Lola's death was filled with small, cramped writing. Augusta didn't have time to read it all now, but she knew Joyce would be interested to see it. She turned to the back of the book where there was a list of addresses. Turning to L for Langley, she found the Cornwall Mansions address in Kensington which Cedric Langley had scarpered from that morning. Was this more evidence Lola had blackmailed him? Why else would she have made a note of his address?

Augusta checked the envelope and saw some papers she had missed. They were neatly folded.

Opening them out, she saw they were bank statements. She flipped through them, looking for large sums of money. And sure enough, she found them. Over the past three months, Lola had deposited three payments of one hundred pounds into her account.

If the payments weren't income from blackmail, then what else could they be?

Chapter 39

BACK AT THE SHOP, Fred was closing up for the day.

'What happened to Philip?' Augusta asked.

'He was called out.'

'To where?'

'He wrote down the address.' Fred went over to the counter and picked up a piece of paper he'd been keeping safe by Sparky's cage. He handed it to Augusta.

'"Cornwall Mansions",' she read out.

'You know it?'

'Yes, it's Cedric Langley's address. We were there first thing this morning. It looks like I'd better get back there again.'

Augusta travelled by taxi and arrived in Kensington twenty minutes later. A constable guarded the door to Mr Langley's building.

'Mr Fisher asked me to come here,' she said. 'Is Detective Sergeant Joyce here as well?'

The constable nodded. 'You'll find them on the third floor, madam.'

Augusta climbed the stairs and found Philip outside a flat on the third floor. The white door to the flat stood ajar and Augusta could hear voices from within.

'Cedric Langley is dead,' said Philip.

'Dead? We saw him only this morning.'

'It's difficult to believe, isn't it? Joyce found him. He came back here this afternoon with a constable to see if Langley was at home after that race around town this morning. When there was no answer, he assumed Langley had taken off somewhere. They broke the door in to have a look round and found him.'

'How horrible. Any sign of Langley's companion?'

'The racing driver? No. The doctor thinks Langley died shortly before Joyce got here. It looks like he was strangled.'

'Like Lola Parker.'

'Very similar.'

'How awful,' said Augusta. 'Someone must have seen something.'

'I hope so,' said Philip. 'There are a lot of flats in these buildings with people coming and going regularly. Joyce has certainly got his work cut out now.'

Detective Sergeant Joyce stepped out of the flat and wiped his brow. 'What a day,' he said.

'How's your leg?' asked Augusta.

'It's alright. Thank you for asking, Mrs Peel. I went to the doctor to get it patched up, then went home to change my trousers. Mrs Joyce isn't very happy about the hole in them. After that, I came here to find out if Cedric Langley had returned. I didn't expect to find him dead. We've got men looking for Langley's companion who drove off with him this morning. He's an obvious suspect. And we've got men calling at all the flats. Hopefully, someone saw the culprit entering or leaving the building.'

'If Langley was strangled, then it's likely it was the same person who attacked Lola Parker,' said Augusta.

'I think so,' said Joyce. 'The method is uncannily similar. Langley was strangled with one of his scarves. We think the attacker took it from one of the pegs in his entrance hall.'

'But he must have known his attacker,' said Philip, 'because he let them in.'

'I think that's likely,' said Joyce. 'Either that, or the attacker forced their way in as soon as he opened the door to them. But I think it's likely he knew them. The person who attacked him and Miss Parker must be someone who was involved with the fashion show.'

Augusta pulled the envelope from Lola's room out of her bag. 'I'm not sure this is of any use now,' she said. 'But I found this beneath Lola Parker's mattress. There's a diary with Langley's address written in it. And bank statements showing she received three large sums of money.'

'How large?' asked Joyce.

'One hundred pounds each time. It supports the theory she was blackmailing Langley, but now we can't know for sure. If only we had happened upon this blackmail theory sooner,' said Augusta. 'We could have asked Langley about it.'

'We tried,' said Joyce, accepting the envelope from her. 'But he ran off.'

'And he may not have been honest with us, anyway,' said Philip. 'Well done on finding the envelope, Augusta. If only the police had found it when they first searched Lola Parker's room.'

'Indeed,' said Joyce, wiping his brow again. 'Thank you for your help, Mrs Peel. I'll have a look through the papers in this envelope, but it may be of no use, as you say. The assailant is keeping one step ahead of us.'

Chapter 40

'WHAT A MYSTERY,' said Fred when Augusta told him about Cedric Langley's murder the following morning. 'It's a shame Detective Sergeant Joyce didn't arrive at Cedric Langley's flat sooner. He could have caught the murderer in the act!'

'He could have.' Augusta sighed. 'I feel like a few opportunities have been missed now. Miss Parker's room wasn't searched properly, and Cedric Langley got away from us yesterday.'

The bell above the shop door rang and Harriet stepped in.

'Fred!' She dashed over to the counter. 'I heard what happened! Are you hurt?'

Augusta retreated to her workshop to give Fred and Harriet some privacy. However, she was keen to hear how Harriet knew Eddie Miller. She continued cleaning the cover of *The Mayor of Casterbridge* and allowed some time to pass.

Harriet had already left when she stepped back into the shop ten minutes later.

'Poor Harriet,' said Fred. 'She blames herself. I told her she mustn't. She apologised for Eddie Miller's behaviour.'

'That's very thoughtful of her,' said Augusta. 'But she needn't apologise on his behalf. He should be the one coming here and apologising.'

'I can't imagine him doing that,' said Fred.

'Did Harriet explain how she knows him?'

'They live on the same street in Clerkenwell. She's known him for a few years. Whenever he sees her, he waves and says hello. Sometimes he tries to have a conversation with her, but she doesn't like him very much. She says she thought he was alright to begin with, but then he asked her if she would like to go to the cinema with him. She didn't want to, and he's become a bit of a nuisance since then.'

'How annoying. He's the sort of man who can't take no for an answer.'

'She says he acts like he has some claim to her,' said Fred. 'And she says she has to avoid him.'

'How did Eddie Miller even know Harriet was chatting to you in this shop?'

'She says he sometimes follows her. Perhaps he looked through the window and saw us talking.'

'He clearly has a habit of pestering young women,' said Augusta. 'He doesn't like it when they turn him down. It makes me wonder what he's capable of.'

Fred's face fell. 'You don't think he could harm Harriet, do you?'

'Hopefully not,' said Augusta, not wishing to worry him. 'He was outside Holland Park Rink on the day of the fashion show. We've got no evidence yet he got into the building and into the changing rooms to harm Lola.'

Fred rubbed his brow. 'But there's a possibility, isn't there? I feel like I should warn Harriet. But I can't, can I? It would completely terrify her.'

'Yes, it would, Fred. It sounds like she's doing quite a good job of looking after herself by distancing herself from him. She clearly tries to avoid him wherever possible. We don't want to scare her so much that she feels afraid. Although Eddie Miller is a suspect in Lola Parker's murder, I really don't see why he would have murdered Cedric Langley. Philip said he would ask someone to keep an eye on Eddie. Hopefully, he won't bother you or Harriet again.'

The shop door opened again and Lady Hereford was pushed inside in her bath chair. 'Oh, Augusta!' she called out. Her nurse wheeled her up to the counter. 'Thank goodness you're here. It's Daphne.'

'What's happened?'

'The police are speaking to her again.'

'So she's been arrested?'

'No. They want to interview her.'

'Again?'

'Yes. Isn't it dreadful? It's to do with the photographer, I forget his name.'

'Cedric Langley.'

'Yes. Him. Apparently, Daphne was with him yesterday.'

Augusta felt her jaw drop. 'Daphne was with him?'

'Yes. She was seen going into his flat yesterday, and now the police think she had something to do with it. Isabella's desperately worried, as you can imagine, Augusta. I'm wondering if you can do the same as you did before and make sure you're with Daphne when she's interviewed by Scotland Yard. I do worry about her. I worry she says silly things sometimes which she'll later regret.'

'Of course I'll be happy to accompany her to the interview,' said Augusta. 'If Detective Sergeant Joyce doesn't mind.'

'I can't believe she's a suspect again!'

'She might not be. The detective will want to interview everybody who saw Cedric Langley yesterday. Daphne may have some helpful information.'

'I don't understand what she was doing there.'

Augusta couldn't understand either. She did her best to calm Lady Hereford. 'She will be able to explain everything, I'm sure.'

'How I wish Daphne would do something sensible with her life! There's something strange about the fashion world. Miss Kingsley seems very odd to me. And everybody involved with it seems so vain. It's a world which brings out the worst in people. And then you end up with this. Murder. Daphne needs to find herself a decent husband and settle down. Rubbing shoulders with all these strange fashion people causes nothing but trouble. And someone could be framing her for these two murders.'

'How would they manage that?'

'I don't know. But someone clever could have put her up to it. Perhaps the murderer suggested to her that she visit Cedric Langley and then the murderer crept in afterwards and murdered him. They would have known full well that Daphne would have been seen entering and leaving the building. I really hope she doesn't get arrested again. She wouldn't cope well with that at all. She hated it last time.'

'Hopefully she won't,' said Augusta. 'I'll telephone Detective Sergeant Joyce and find out when he's planning to speak to her. I'll do what I can to be there.'

'Thank you, Augusta.' Lady Hereford reached out and clasped her hand. 'I'm very grateful to you.'

Chapter 41

DAPHNE'S EYES were rimmed with red. Her face looked freshly powdered, and she wore a lilac dress with billowing sleeves and a pleated skirt. A pendant around her neck caught Augusta's eye. It was a small enamel jewelled egg, similar to the one she had seen in Lola's room.

'I don't understand why I'm here,' said Daphne, dabbing her eyes. They sat with Detective Sergeant Joyce in the small interview room at Kensington police station.

'What time did you visit Cedric Langley?' the detective asked. He clearly didn't want to waste time explaining to Daphne why she was being interviewed.

'It was just after lunchtime,' she said. 'I wanted to see some photographs he took of me.'

'What time was "just after lunchtime"?'

'About two o'clock. But I can't be absolutely certain about that. It was roughly that time.'

'So you were in his flat at two o'clock yesterday?'

'Around that time. Yes.'

'Was there anyone else in the flat?'

'No, it was just me and Cedric.'

'And how was he?'

'He was fine. He was expecting me because I'd already told him I would like to see the photographs.'

'Why weren't the photographs in his studio?'

'I don't know. He told me they were at his flat.'

'Did anything appear to be bothering him when you saw him?'

'No. But I wouldn't know for sure. I didn't know him that well.'

'And how long were you at his flat for?'

'Not long. About twenty minutes. I'd arranged to meet my mother for a shopping trip.'

'So you left at what time?'

'Well. About twenty past two.'

'Did Mr Langley mention what he was going to be doing for the rest of the day?'

'No. He showed me the photographs, and that was that. I had no idea it would be the last time I saw him.' She dissolved into tears. 'I know what this looks like,' she said when she recovered herself. 'You've already arrested me once. You think I did this, don't you? Because I saw Cedric Langley on the day he died, you think I murdered him. I had nothing to do with this. I promise!'

'I haven't made my mind up yet,' said Detective Sergeant Joyce. 'All I'm trying to do at the moment is speak to everyone who saw him yesterday. Did he mention anyone else would be visiting him that day?'

'No. And I wish he had! Then I could help you. I don't understand why this has happened. Two people dead, and both of them strangled. Why would someone do this to Lola and Cedric? It makes no sense!'

'What was the relationship like between Miss Parker and Mr Langley?'

'Oh, I don't know. They weren't especially friendly with

each other, as far as I was aware. I think she annoyed him a little bit because she used to get a bit bored during the photography sessions. But I think Lola liked Mr Langley. There was a lot to like about him, really. That's why I don't understand this. Everyone seemed to like him. Why would someone harm him?'

'That's what we want to find out.'

'I hope you find the person who did this,' said Daphne. 'And then I won't be blamed for it. But if you don't find the person, then you're going to arrest me, aren't you? I know it!'

'No, Daphne, it's just unfortunate that you happened to be in the vicinity when two murders were committed.'

'Completely unfortunate! It's not fair! How I wish I could turn the clock back and make sure I wasn't there at all!'

Isabella Chatsworth was waiting for her daughter in the reception area once the interview had finished. 'Oh Daphne, have you told them everything you know?' She embraced her daughter.

'Yes, Mother.'

'It's all so dreadful.'

'Mrs Chatsworth,' said Detective Sergeant Joyce. 'Did you see your daughter yesterday?'

'Yes.'

'Where and what time?'

'We met outside Bond Street tube station at three o'clock.'

'Thank you.'

'Why do you ask, Detective?'

'I'm just establishing your daughter's whereabouts yesterday.'

'Then I shall elaborate, Detective. After some shopping, we travelled home by tube to Richmond. We got home about quarter past six. Does that answer your question, Detective?'

'Quite adequately. Thank you, Mrs Chatsworth.'

She gave him a sharp look before escorting her daughter from the building.

'What did you make of that?' Augusta asked Joyce once they had left.

'The young woman seems honest enough. But we can't ignore the fact she was in the proximity of both murders.'

'I can't think of a motive for Daphne murdering either of them.'

'Neither can I. It's probably just a case of being in the wrong place at the wrong time. Twice.' He scratched his chin. 'We shall continue our enquiries. In the meantime, a gentleman handed himself in to this station late last night. He identified himself as Mr Graham Crowley, a friend of Mr Langley's and the chap who sped off in the Vauxhall yesterday morning. He spoke to Inspector Willis here and told him he'd heard about Langley's death from friends. He was extremely upset and wanted to make it clear he had nothing to do with it. He knew the police would be looking for him, so he handed himself in and, in his words, wanted to be honest about why he drove off like that.'

'And what was his reason?' asked Augusta.

'He said he and Langley panicked. They'd noticed us there and were worried about being seen together. When you consider the rumour about Langley and the son of a duke, they were understandably worried about being arrested. Speeding off in a motor car was not an appropriate response, however. Willis told me Crowley apologised profusely for his actions and both he and Langley regretted what they did.'

'Presumably they returned to Langley's flat after they lost us.'

'Yes, Crowley said he dropped Langley off there at one o'clock and went on his way. That ties in with what Miss Chatsworth told us. She arrived at Langley's flat at two and he was alive and well at that time. She also maintains she left him alive and well twenty minutes later. Then I got there shortly after three.'

'When he was neither alive nor well.'

'Not at all. So Miss Chatsworth could be lying. Or Crowley could have returned and murdered his friend. Or another person unknown to us did it.'

'Did Inspector Willis give you his opinion of Crowley?'

'He told me he was repentant and saddened by the death of his friend. He said he seemed sincere and keen for the culprit to be caught. Following Crowley's confession, Willis arrested him for driving a motor car to the danger of the public. He was due to be in front of the magistrates for that this morning.' Joyce shook his head. 'It's a silly state of affairs. If Langley hadn't taken off like that, we could have interviewed him here at the station about the blackmail. If he'd been here and not in his flat, then his murderer wouldn't have called on him. The chap could've been still alive!'

Chapter 42

'You've just missed Detective Inspector Morris,' said Philip when Augusta returned to her shop.

'Good,' she said. 'I'm still annoyed with him for failing to notice the rear door to Briggs's office.'

'Ah yes, well, let's forget about that now. Morris has received some intelligence about the painting *Sunset at the Temple of Artemis*.'

'Is it reliable intelligence?'

'Yes. Morris has heard Briggs is hiding his stolen paintings in private homes.'

'Do the people who live in the homes know the paintings are stolen?'

'No. And they think they're merely borrowing the artworks from him in return for a fee.'

'So they're paying Briggs to look after his stolen art for him?'

'Yes. Apparently, he tells them they can hang the paintings in their homes while he looks for suitable buyers.'

Augusta shook her head. 'I'm astonished at what he gets away with.'

'So am I. We need to stop him!'

'We? What about your family, Philip? He's threatened them.'

'And they're being looked after by the police in Bognor. The sooner we find this painting, the sooner he's arrested and then my family is safe again. Do you see?'

'I think so.'

'Morris says *Sunset at the Temple of Artemis* is believed to be at Holland House in Kensington.'

'And who lives at Holland House?' asked Augusta.

'Lord and Lady Whittington.'

'And what does he know about them?'

'Not a lot.'

'Why doesn't Morris just go in there with his men and seize the painting?'

'They're not certain it's there.'

'I thought you said the intelligence was reliable.'

'It is. Well, about as reliable as a word from a police informer can be. Morris is worried if they charge in there to get the painting and it's not there, then Briggs will hear of the police raid and go to more lengths to hide all his stolen artwork.'

'I see. So Morris wants us to have a look in Holland House.'

'He wants someone to.'

'But you think we could do it. It's not going to be easy for us to walk in there, is it?'

'No. We shall have to think of a way of doing it undercover. And not as Mr and Mrs Dennis of West Norwood. They're dead now and their bodies have been left in a ditch in Kent.'

'Whose bodies?' asked Fred with a shocked expression. He had been reorganising some shelves nearby.

'Don't worry, Fred,' said Augusta. 'Mr and Mrs Dennis never existed.'

'Oh.'

'We need to get into Holland House to see if there's a stolen painting on display there,' said Augusta. 'We know Lord and Lady Whittington live there, but that's about it.'

'I could find out more about them,' said Fred. 'My Mother has an extensive collection of *Aristo* magazines, remember?'

Aristo was a high society publication which featured news and photographs of all the important people.

'And I can have a look in *Burke's Peerage* in Holborn Library on my way home,' said Fred.

'Some more information on the Whittingtons would be very useful,' said Augusta. 'Thank you, Fred.'

Chapter 43

AUGUSTA WAS ARRIVING at her shop the following morning when she caught sight of a young woman running along the street towards her.

'Mrs Peel!'

It was Daphne Chatsworth. Her hair was in her eyes and her handbag was slipping off her shoulder.

'What's wrong?'

'Oh, Mrs Peel. I've been sent something horrible in the post!'

'Goodness. You'd better come in.'

Fred had already opened the shop for the day. He greeted them, and Augusta placed Sparky's cage on the counter. 'Miss Chatsworth needs to speak to me about something,' she said. 'We'll go into the workshop.'

In the workshop, Augusta pulled out a stool for Daphne to sit on. 'What's arrived in the post?' she asked.

Daphne put an envelope on the worktable. Augusta could see Daphne's Richmond address on it. The envelope had been opened.

'Who's it from?' Augusta asked.

'I don't know! Look inside!'

Augusta cautiously picked up the envelope, unsure about what she was going to find. There was a note inside and a red and gold silk scarf which had been neatly folded.

Augusta unfolded the note. Just two words were written on it: "You're next."

'I see what you mean,' she said. 'It's horrible indeed.'

Augusta unfolded the scarf. It was printed with a gold geometric design.

'I recognise the scarf,' sniffed Daphne. 'It's a Kingsley one.'

'You've seen someone wearing it?'

'No. But I recognise it from the latest collection, and you can look at the label to see it's Kingsley.'

Augusta examined the postmark on the envelope. 'It looks like this was posted near Oxford Circus,' she said.

'I noticed that.'

'Can you think of anyone who lives or works in that area?'

'The Kingsley boutique is nearby.'

'You think Miss Kingsley could have sent you this?'

'No,' said Daphne. 'That would be too obvious, wouldn't it? If she sent me one of her own scarves and threatened me, then she'd just be giving herself away, wouldn't she? I think someone chose this scarf because they know I work as a model for Miss Kingsley. And because Lola was strangled by a Kingsley scarf. As for Cedric, I don't know what type of scarf he was wearing. But it's someone who knows something about the crimes, isn't it? It must be the murderer!'

'Why would they come for you next?'

'I've no idea!'

Augusta refolded the scarf as she thought. To her knowledge, Lola and Cedric had not been sent warnings before their deaths. So why had Daphne received one? Was it someone's idea of a joke?

'I think you need to take this to Scotland Yard and show Detective Sergeant Joyce,' said Augusta. 'Do you recognise the handwriting at all?'

'No, I don't. But if it's someone I know, then they're going to disguise their handwriting, aren't they?'

'I'll telephone Detective Sergeant Joyce,' said Augusta. 'And arrange for you to hand this over to him. But I think this could be a sinister prank of some sort. If someone really wanted to harm you, they wouldn't warn you, would they?'

'Maybe not,' said Daphne. 'But they're trying to frighten me. Why would they do that? I've done nothing wrong!'

Chapter 44

Vivien Kingsley marched into her office where her assistant Miss Bilston and Nikolai were waiting for her.

'The seamstresses are behind,' she announced, striding over to her desk. 'I've told them they'll have to work over the weekend. They don't like it, but we have no choice. The collection needs to be finished on time. Do you know what their excuse is? Apparently, some of the embroidery is too intricate. But I discussed it with Mary when we were planning out the schedule and she told me how many weeks it would take. So they can't complain to me it's more intricate than they were expecting. I based my entire plan around Mary's estimate.' She noticed Miss Bilston looked paler than usual. 'Is something wrong, Miss Bilston?'

'I've just opened your morning's post, Miss Kingsley. And there was something which is rather concerning.'

'What is it?'

'It's probably best if you don't see it and I'll just report it to the police.'

'Report what to the police? What are you talking about, Miss Bilston?'

'It's probably just someone being strange.'

'Can I see it, please?'

'I don't think it's a good idea.'

'I shall decide whether or not it's a good idea. Now hand it over.'

Miss Bilston got up from her seat and handed her an envelope. Vivien peered into it. 'It looks like one of my Sunburst scarves,' she said. 'Why has someone sent me one of my own scarves?' Then she noticed a small piece of paper folded in with it.

She pulled it out and opened it. A chill grew in her stomach as she read the few words: "You're next."

'Oh.' She dropped everything onto her desk. 'I see what you mean now, Miss Bilston.'

'I'm sorry, Miss Kingsley, I didn't want you to see it.'

'What does it say?' asked Nikolai, getting to his feet.

'It's just a silly note, Nikolai,' said Vivien. 'Someone playing a prank.'

He stepped over to the desk and read the note. 'You're next? Does someone want to murder you?'

Vivien shivered. 'No. They're only joking. But we should tell the police all the same.'

'I want to find out who did this!' said Nikolai.

'We all do. But let's leave it to the police.' She folded up the note and pushed it back into the envelope with the scarf. 'Take this down to the nearest police station please, Miss Bilston.' She held it out to her. 'Someone seems to think they can frighten me. That's because they don't know me at all!' She gave a laugh, but she could feel her hands trembling.

Chapter 45

'I HAD a good look through my mother's *Aristo* magazines and found a few mentions of Lord and Lady Whittington,' said Fred. He placed the magazines on the counter. Augusta could see he'd marked the relevant pages with little strips of paper.

'Thank you, Fred. It must have taken you all evening.'

'I don't mind. I quite enjoyed it.' He turned to the first marked page. 'Here they are at a ball at the Dorchester Hotel.' Augusta peered at the photograph to see a couple in their sixties. They had imperious expressions and wore their finest evening wear. 'And here they are at a dinner with the Prime Minister.' Augusta surveyed the line of dignitaries. The men looked like penguins in their dinner suits and the ladies glittered with jewels. 'Their charitable work is mentioned quite a bit,' said Fred.

'Which is a good sign of someone putting their wealth and status to good use,' said Augusta. 'What sort of charity work do they support?'

'They've hosted dinners to raise money for West London Hospital.'

'That's nice of them.' An idea formed in her mind.

Fred cleared his throat. 'I also found this.' He picked up another magazine and turned to a spread of photographs which he had marked. 'These were taken at the races last month,' he said. 'The caption to this one refers to the Earl of Uppingham and his daughter, Lady Amesbury.'

Augusta took in a breath.

Her father and sister.

They stood together in the bright sunshine, smiling at the photographer. Her father wore a top hat and held a pair of gloves in his hand. Her sister wore a large summer hat and light-coloured dress with bows and ribbons on the bodice and a sheer layer of fabric over the skirt.

Augusta was struck by the familiarity of her father's face, although it was a little more gaunt and lined than in the last photograph she had seen of him. Her sister had changed little. They had never got on well.

'I'm sorry, Augusta,' said Fred. 'Maybe it was a mistake to point this out to you. It's just when I learned about your family, I was surprised to see this. Or perhaps I wasn't surprised, after all, they're the sort of family to be photographed in *Aristo* magazine, I suppose.'

'Please don't worry, Fred,' said Augusta. 'Thank you for pointing out the photograph to me. This is the first photograph I've seen of them for some time,' she said. 'It's nice to see they're happy.'

'They seem so,' said Fred.

Augusta wondered if her father ever gave her much thought. Or had he forgotten about her completely? She pushed the thought away. She had managed for twenty years having nothing to do with him. There was no use in considering what could have been.

'Thank you for your research into the Whittingtons, Fred,' said Augusta. 'I think I have a good idea now how we can approach them.'

Chapter 46

THAT AFTERNOON, Augusta and Philip sat with Detective Sergeant Joyce in his office at Scotland Yard. On his desk in front of him were two scarves, and two envelopes, and two notes.

'So Daphne Chatsworth and Miss Kingsley have both received identical threatening letters,' said Detective Sergeant Joyce. 'Both were posted in the Oxford Circus area of London yesterday evening. The trouble is, with Cedric Langley now dead, we're running out of suspects.'

'The only person who comes to mind is Eddie Miller,' said Philip.

'He's a possibility,' said Detective Sergeant Joyce. 'But the most obvious question is, why would he do it?'

'We can establish a motive for why he attacked Miss Parker,' said Augusta. 'But we don't know why he would have murdered Mr Langley. Or why he would then threaten Miss Kingsley and Miss Chatsworth. How did he even know their addresses?'

'Indeed,' said Detective Sergeant Joyce. 'Having spoken

to the young man in question, he doesn't strike me as the cleverest of fellows. Perhaps I'm wrong.'

'No, I don't think you're wrong, Joyce,' said Philip. 'I don't think he would be clever enough to find out the addresses of Miss Kingsley and Miss Chatsworth. For one thing, he's never even met Miss Kingsley, surely? And does he even know who Miss Chatsworth is? He may never have met her either.'

'Perhaps he's cleverer than we think,' said Augusta. 'Miss Parker's murder was widely reported in the newspapers. Perhaps he read the names mentioned in the reports and somehow found out the addresses of the people involved. He could have looked them up in a directory. So I don't think he's incapable of doing this, but I don't understand his reason why.'

'A grudge against the fashion house?' said Detective Sergeant Joyce.

'It certainly looks like a grudge against the fashion house,' said Philip. 'But why would Eddie Miller hold such a grudge? We know he possibly bore a grudge against Miss Parker, but the whole fashion house? That suggests a rather disordered way of thinking.'

'But not impossible,' said Augusta. 'The only other possibility is there's a suspect we haven't considered yet. If the motive is a grudge against the fashion house, then perhaps the murderer is someone from a rival fashion house?'

'If it's someone we've not even considered yet, then we have to start this investigation all over again,' said Detective Sergeant Joyce. He gave a weary sigh. 'I suppose there could have been people from rival fashion houses at the fashion show that afternoon. It makes sense they would have been there. They would have been interested to see Miss Kingsley's collection, no doubt.'

'Yes, that must be a possibility,' said Philip. 'Surely there will be something in the records of the ticket sales?'

'I'll ask to have a look at them,' said Detective Sergeant Joyce. 'And then I can speak to anyone who was there from a rival fashion house. You would have thought if there had been a fierce rivalry, Miss Kingsley would have mentioned it. I've spoken to her about this letter and she can't think of anyone who bears her a grudge.'

'But in the meantime, she and Miss Chatsworth are going to have to be careful about where they go and who they spend time with,' said Philip. 'It seems this assailant is running rings around us all.'

Chapter 47

AUGUSTA AND PHILIP walked up the driveway of Holland House the following day. The late summer sun shone on the red brick of the impressive home. It was in the Jacobean style, with curved gables, stone mullion windows and two turrets with steeply pitched roofs.

'You could live in a place like this, Augusta,' said Philip.

She laughed. 'I don't think so!'

'Yes, you could. You could renounce your ordinariness and revert to your true name, Lady Rebecca Buchanan. Then you could marry the heir to a family which has a house like this.'

'And I would have everlasting happiness?'

'Of course.'

She laughed. 'I think I'd be quite fed up living in a house like this. I've heard it's difficult to recruit enough servants these days.'

'What a terrible problem to have.'

Augusta wondered if Philip thought about the moment they had almost kissed. The worry about the threat to his wife and son had extinguished any hope of it happening again. Augusta had been reminded of how important they were to him. Perhaps Philip still loved his wife.

A maid answered the door.

'Good morning,' said Augusta. 'We're Mr and Mrs Marshall, and we're representatives of the Fulham Children's Hospital. We rely on the kind assistance of well-meaning patrons. We're wondering if Lord and Lady Whittington might like to hear a little more about our work?'

'Lord Whittington is away,' said the maid. 'Lady Whittington is at home. She doesn't usually receive callers in the morning, but I shall speak with her. Do you have visiting cards?'

'I'm afraid we don't. It's quite an expense to have them printed, and we like to spare as many funds as we can for the hospital.'

'I see.'

The maid invited them into the entrance hall and went off for a short while. Augusta and Philip admired the large portraits on the wall.

'You're probably related to some of these people, Augusta,' whispered Philip.

'Oh, shush!'

The maid returned. 'Lady Whittington will see you now.'

Lady Whittington received them in a large sitting room. She stood by the fireplace, leaning on a walking stick. She greeted them with a smile.

'Another person who needs assistance walking,' she said to Philip. 'My incapacity is my age. However, my guess is you were injured during the war.'

Philip nodded. 'That's right, my lady.'

'How frustrating for a young man like yourself.'

'Yes, it is frustrating. I wouldn't describe myself as young, though.'

'You're young compared to me.' She gestured at the many chairs in the room. 'Please make yourself comfortable. I hear you're from the hospital charity.'

'Yes, that's right,' said Philip.

Lady Whittington appeared to have taken a shine to Philip, which Augusta was pleased about. This meant he could distract her while Augusta found an opportunity to sneak off and look for the painting.

Philip gave a small speech on the work of the fictional hospital and Lady Whittington nodded as he spoke, keenly interested in every word he was saying. Augusta felt a pang of guilt that they were lying to her. She reassured herself they were doing it so Lord Montpelier could be reunited with his painting. And Briggs could be arrested and hopefully the other stolen artworks could be recovered too.

After Philip had spoken for five minutes, Augusta asked if she could excuse herself to use the bathroom.

'Of course,' said Lady Whittington. She rang a little bell on the occasional table next to her chair and the maid appeared.

'Maisie, please will you show Mrs Marshall to the nearest bathroom?'

Maisie nodded and Augusta followed her.

'Would you like me to wait for you, Mrs Marshall? Or do you think you'll be able to find your way back?'

'Thank you, but I'll be able to find my way back, no problem at all,' said Augusta.

Maisie went on her way and Augusta went into the bathroom and waited for a minute. She reasoned *Sunset at the Temple of Artemis* would be displayed in a prominent location in one of the rooms. Perhaps a room which the Whittingtons liked to entertain in.

She listened carefully at the door. Everything seemed silent beyond it. She opened the door and peered out into the corridor. There was no one around.

Augusta crept to the entrance hall, then she crossed in front of the staircase and headed for a door which stood ajar. She peered in to see the drawing room. It was tastefully furnished and there were pictures on the wall, but none of them was the picture she was looking for.

Checking around her again, she moved along to the next door. It was shut. She held her breath, turned the handle as carefully as possible, and prayed that it didn't creak. The door opened out into the library. The walls were lined with bookshelves and there was only space for a few small paintings.

Augusta quietly shut the door again and continued to the next door. Her heart thudded in her chest. She had been away from Philip and Lady Whittington for over five minutes. She hoped Lady Whittington wasn't wondering where she was.

She tried the handle of the next door and found the billiard room. There was no sign of the painting. Augusta was just about to make her way further along the corridor when she heard footsteps advancing. She didn't want to be challenged. She made her way back to the billiards room, opened the door and quickly stepped inside. The footsteps marched past on the tiled floor. Her breath eased as she listened to the footsteps die away. Then she left the billiards room, checked there was no one around and went on to the next door. This door stood slightly ajar.

Inside the room, a large dining table was surrounded by two dozen chairs. The oak-panelled room had two windows which looked out over parkland. She turned to look at the fireplace and grinned as she saw the large painting hanging above it. It depicted a ruined classical temple with three nymph-like women and a dramatic sunset.

She was just about to leave the room when she heard footsteps in the corridor again. Augusta dropped to her hands and knees and crawled beneath the enormous dining table.

She was just in time as she saw two pairs of feet enter the room.

Chapter 48

'I'D LIKE to know if you know anything about the china cherub ornament which was broken in the library yesterday, Nelly,' said a woman's voice.

Augusta tried to breathe as quietly as possible as she hid beneath the table.

'No, Mrs Cousins. I don't know nothing about it.'

'It was clearly knocked off the shelf and broke,' said Mrs Cousins, 'and then it was placed back on the shelf in the hope no one would notice the breakage. You are aware that all breakages must be reported to me?'

Augusta guessed Mrs Cousins was the housekeeper and poor Nelly was a maid.

'I don't know nothing about it, Mrs Cousins.'

'But you must know something about it, Nelly. You were dusting in the library yesterday.'

'The ornaments looked alright to me then, Mrs Cousins.'

'They can't have been.'

'But it wasn't me, Mrs Cousins,' Augusta could hear a

hint of upset in Nelly's voice. She hoped the discussion would soon finish. But Mrs Cousins was insistent.

'We're not leaving this room, Nelly, until you explain to me what happened.'

'Nothing happened, Mrs Cousins. I dusted the room, but I didn't knock the cherub off the shelf and break it. I would have come to you if that had happened.'

'You are aware it's an extremely valuable ornament?'

'Yes, I'm aware of that, Mrs Cousins. And that's why I would have told you if it had been me who'd knocked it off the shelf. But when I was dusting, I moved the cherub to dust around it and replaced it. It wasn't broken then. Someone must have come into the room after me and broken it.'

'And how would they have managed that?'

'I don't know, Mrs Cousins. But it wasn't me. Maybe Mr Wilkins needed to change the time on the clock and he knocked it then.'

'I can scarcely believe what I'm hearing, Nelly. Are you seriously accusing the butler of knocking the cherub ornament off the shelf and not informing anyone about it?'

'No, I'm not accusing him, Mrs Cousins. I don't even know if he changed the time on the clock yesterday. But I was just trying to think of how someone else could have knocked it.'

Augusta's knees ached. What would Philip be thinking now? She had been gone from the room for at least ten minutes.

The discussion continued. The housekeeper was keen to get a confession from Nelly, but she got nowhere.

'I shall report back to Lady Whittington,' said Mrs Cousins. 'And I shall let her decide whether or not she docks your wages for the cost of repairs.'

There was a long pause. Then Augusta heard the sound of sobbing.

'Oh, for goodness sake, pull yourself together, Nelly. I've not got time for your tears now. You've only got yourself to blame.'

'But I didn't do anything.'

Augusta felt sorry for Nelly. The girl had been so insistent she hadn't broken the cherub ornament that Augusta was inclined to believe her. She felt tempted to crawl out from beneath the dining table and defend the poor maid. But she had to stay out of it.

'Dry your eyes and get on with your work now, please, Nelly,' said the housekeeper. 'I don't want another word from you for the rest of the day.'

The dining room door opened and closed again. Mrs Cousins had left the room, but Augusta could still hear sobbing.

Carefully and slowly, she crawled out from beneath the table. Nelly stood near the door, drying her eyes on her apron. She gave a gasp when she saw Augusta, but Augusta immediately put her finger to her lips.

'Don't be alarmed,' she said. 'I'm supposed to be in the sitting room with Lady Whittington. I went to the bathroom and lost my way. I came in here but then heard you and Mrs Cousins behind me. I thought it was best I hid. It was very silly of me, I realise that. I don't know what happened with the ornament, Nelly, but I don't think it's fair you should have to pay for it to be repaired.' She pulled out one of her cards from her handbag.

'If they make you pay for the ornament, then just contact me.'

The maid said nothing but stared at her open-mouthed.

'Here, take this,' said Augusta. 'It's got my phone

number on it. Don't tell anybody I gave my card to you and don't tell anybody you saw me here. And in return for you keeping quiet, I shall pay for the ornament for you.'

'But it's not fair you should pay for it,' said Nelly.

'I'd much rather pay for it than know you're struggling to do so,' said Augusta. 'I know this looks a little odd, me being here. But let's both agree to keep the whole matter quiet, shall we?'

Nelly nodded.

'And if Mrs Cousins keeps treating you like this, I'm sure you can find work in another place,' said Augusta. 'There are lots of vacancies for maids in London. All the big houses struggle to recruit staff these days.'

The girl nodded. 'I've been thinking about that,' she said. 'Mrs Cousins has always got it in for me.'

'Well, she's in the wrong,' said Augusta. 'I shall return now to see Lady Whittington. I shall have to explain I got lost on the way back from the bathroom.'

They exchanged a smile and Augusta went on her way.

Augusta had a skip in her step as she returned to the sitting room. *Sunset at the Temple of Artemis* had been found. But poor Lady Whittington had no idea it had been stolen. She was in for a shock.

'Did you get lost?' asked Lady Whittington when Augusta returned to the sitting room.

'Yes, I'm afraid I did,' said Augusta. 'It was very foolish of me. For some reason, I thought the sitting room was on the other side of the staircase. I don't know how I managed it, but thankfully a very helpful maid called Nelly showed me the right way.'

'Nelly helped you, did she? I'm pleased to hear it.'

'I think I've just about finished telling Lady Whittington all about the charity,' said Philip. He forced a smile.

'Have you? I'm sorry I missed most of it.'

'No, I don't think you're finished at all, Mr Marshall,' said Lady Whittington with a grin. 'How about some more tea?'

They left Holland House half an hour later.

'Well done, Philip,' said Augusta. 'It's quite clear Lady Whittington likes you.'

'It was rather hard to get away, wasn't it? Now tell me what went on, Augusta. You were gone for ages.'

'The painting's in there! It's in the dining room. I had just spotted it, and then I had to hide under the dining table because the housekeeper brought in a maid to tell her off.'

'And you're sure it's Lord Montpelier's stolen painting?'

'Very sure.'

'Wonderful news. I shall tell Morris. Poor Lady Whittington. She's a pleasant lady. I feel quite ashamed that I've spent all that time with her talking about a fictitious hospital.'

'She should know better than to deal with someone like Briggs,' said Augusta. 'Just a few minutes in his company is enough to convince anyone he's no good.'

'Well, Morris can visit the Whittingtons tomorrow and ask them all about the dealer they're paying to borrow the painting. They'll land Briggs right in it!'

Chapter 49

The Mayor of Casterbridge was finally cleaned up. Augusta showed the book to Fred.

'It looks wonderful,' he said. 'We should sell it for two shillings and sixpence.'

'But that's what we sold *Bleak House* for, and it's shorter than *Bleak House*.'

'But it's a classic book, and it's in excellent condition now you've repaired it. And Harriet mentioned she'd like to read some more of Thomas Hardy's books.'

'If Harriet wants to buy it, then you must offer her a discount.'

'She would appreciate that. She's spent quite a lot of money here recently.'

'I wonder why that is?' Augusta gave him a knowing smile, and he looked bashful.

The ring of the telephone interrupted them.

'Mrs Peel?' said the lady's voice on the other end. 'This is Miss Bilston, Miss Kingsley's assistant. I hope you don't mind me telephoning you. I've been doing quite a bit of thinking, and I'd like to discuss something with you.'

'Of course. What would you like to discuss?'

'Well, it's a person, actually. Someone who bothers me quite a bit.'

'Who's bothering you, Miss Bilston?'

'Nikolai Volkov.'

Chapter 50

'IT SOUNDS like we need to visit Miss Kingsley,' said Philip after Augusta had told him about her conversation with Miss Bilston. 'I'll telephone Joyce and ask him to meet us at the Kingsley boutique.'

Later that afternoon, Augusta and Philip sat with Detective Sergeant Joyce in Miss Kingsley's apartment.

'Where's Mr Volkov?' Joyce asked the fashion designer.

'I don't know. I'm not his keeper!' The stack of bracelets on her arm jingled as she lit a cigarette. 'Why do you want to speak to him, anyway?' she continued. 'What's he done?'

'I'm not entirely sure yet.' Detective Sergeant Joyce turned to Augusta. 'Perhaps you can explain, Mrs Peel.'

'Lola Parker's flatmate, Mabel Roberts, suspected Lola had a secret boyfriend,' said Augusta. 'But she didn't know who he was. Lola was very secretive about him. Lola didn't want anybody knowing the identity of her boyfriend, and I suspect he didn't want anybody knowing either. I think that could be because he was already in a relationship with someone else. Then today I received a telephone call from Miss Bilston. She wanted to speak to me about Mr Volkov.'

'That's because Miss Bilston hates Nikolai,' said Miss Kingsley.

'May I ask why?'

'Because he's often hanging about here, getting in the way. He doesn't do anything useful.'

Augusta continued. 'Miss Bilston told me she overheard an argument between you, Miss Kingsley, and Mr Volkov.'

'Oh, did she? I don't see why she had to telephone you and tell you about my personal affairs.'

'From what she overheard, Miss Bilston got the impression you had discovered Mr Volkov had been having an affair.'

Miss Kingsley laughed. 'I can just picture her with her ear at the door enjoying that conversation!'

'Was Mr Volkov having an affair?' asked Philip.

'It's no one's business!'

'I'm afraid it is when it's linked to murder, Miss Kingsley,' said Detective Sergeant Joyce. 'I think now is the time to stop making excuses for yourself and tell us the truth, Miss Kingsley. Did you suspect Mr Volkov was having an affair and did you confront him about it?'

'How do you know this has anything to do with murder?'

'Please just tell us the truth, Miss Kingsley,' said Philip. 'This has gone on long enough.'

'Fine! I'll tell you what happened. But it's irrelevant to your investigation. I haven't murdered anyone, and neither has Nikolai.' She sighed and rubbed her brow. 'I grew suspicious of him. His behaviour changed and his manner towards me was different. You can just tell. He was going out more without me. There were nights and excuses made when I wanted us to do something together. He seemed distracted and less interested in me. And then I discovered he lied to me about where he'd been one evening. So, yes. I confronted him. I had no idea Miss Bilston was listening in and I'm mortified she told Mrs Peel about it. But there you go. That's the truth.'

'Did he admit it?' asked Augusta.

'Of course he didn't admit it. Men never do, do they? They deny these things for as long as they can get away with it. But I knew.'

'Do you know who he was having an affair with?' asked Joyce.

'No.'

'That's rather convenient of you to say that, isn't it, Miss Kingsley? Because if you knew he was having an affair with Lola Parker, that would give you a motive to murder her, wouldn't it?'

'Absolutely not!'

'Are you quite sure you didn't know it was Miss Parker?'

'I didn't know who it was!'

'Because if you had discovered that Miss Parker was having an affair with your boyfriend, then you would have confronted her, wouldn't you? And perhaps the confrontation would have become nasty.'

'Even if I had found out his affair was with Lola, I wouldn't have murdered her. I may be lots of things, Detective, but I'm not a killer. I can tell by your expression that you don't believe me, but it's the truth. What you don't understand is that I've been here before. Way too many times before!' She laughed again and puffed out a cloud of smoke. 'I've had a lot of boyfriends over the years. I'm not ashamed to admit that. Men are drawn to me because of my fame and success. But once they realise that behind the veneer is just a normal woman, they lose interest.'

Miss Kingsley suddenly seemed rather fragile. Augusta felt a bit sorry for her.

'Who doesn't want to be loved?' She forced a smile. 'My trouble is I always pick the wrong sort of man. I never expected this relationship to last forever. Nikolai is handsome, and he was good company for a while. It was fun while it lasted.'

'Did you plan to end the relationship?' asked Augusta.

'I wasn't sure what to do. Although I felt sure he was lying, I also knew there was a possibility I was mistaken. To be honest, I can't fully explain my thoughts at the time. I was upset and I felt confused about it. If I'd had evidence of Nikolai's affair, then that would have been the end of us. I planned to look for more evidence of the affair. But it's safe to say our relationship was nearing its end.'

'Did Nikolai know that?' asked Detective Sergeant Joyce.

'No. Obviously, he knew I was angry and upset with him. He tried to make things better by buying me gifts. That's what Nikolai does. He's very good at buying gifts. I can't deny I like gifts, but I'd much rather have fidelity.'

'Do you think Nikolai was fearful of you discovering evidence of his affair?'

'I don't know if fearful is the right word to use, but he was probably worried that I would be proven right.'

'Perhaps he tried to cover his tracks?'

'Well, I suppose that's a possibility. He could have done.'

'What would it have meant to him if you had ended the relationship?'

'I think he would have been upset. And it would have

been a blow to his popularity. All our friends would have sided with me.'

'He would have lost influential friends?'

'Yes, definitely. He didn't know many people when he first came to England. My friendships and connections with important people were valuable to him. So yes, he would have lost all those friendships once people discovered he'd been unfaithful. He would have probably had to go off to Paris or somewhere and start again from there.'

'So you think it's possible Mr Volkov would have done anything to make sure you didn't find out about the affair?' said Philip. 'He didn't want to lose his valuable friendships, and he didn't want to lose his status of being associated with you, one of the most famous fashion designers in the world.'

'I don't think I'm that famous! But as you put it like that, Mr Fisher, I shall agree with you. It would have mattered a great deal to him.'

Augusta noticed her face change a little. As if she had suddenly realised what she was implying.

'So Mr Volkov would have been worried after you confronted him,' said Philip. 'He wouldn't have wanted any evidence of his affair to be discovered. So it makes sense that he sought to get rid of the evidence.'

'No,' said Miss Kingsley. 'That's not right at all.'

'Why not? You've already explained to us it would have mattered to him a great deal if you had ended the relationship. He would have lost his status here in London. He needed you.'

'Are you suggesting his affair was with Lola and he murdered her to shush it up? You're very much mistaken. There's no way he would have done such a thing. Nikolai is not a murderer!'

The apartment door opened and Nikolai Volkov

stepped in. 'Oh I'm sorry, Vivien. I didn't realise you had company.' He moved to leave the room again.

'Come and sit down, Nikolai, and explain yourself,' said Miss Kingsley. 'These three are accusing you of murder!'

Chapter 51

Nikolai Volkov perched himself in an antique chair and gave everyone a wary glance.

Detective Sergeant Joyce asked the first question. 'Did you have an affair with Lola Parker, Mr Volkov?'

'No.'

'Oh, just tell everyone the truth, Nikolai!' said Miss Kingsley, hurling a brocade cushion at him. It hit him on the shoulder and landed on the floor. 'I'm tired of your lies!'

'Alright then,' he said. 'I did.'

'Miss Kingsley suspected you of having an affair, didn't she?' asked Joyce.

'Yes.'

'And you denied it.'

'Yes.'

'If you had admitted the affair, then she would have ended the relationship. You would have had a fall from grace, wouldn't you? You would have lost all your new, powerful friends.'

Nikolai shrugged. 'I don't know.'

'Lola Parker could have told someone about your affair, couldn't she?'

'I asked her not to.'

'Why?'

'Because she would have found out.'

'She?'

'Miss Kingsley.'

'You didn't want her to find out, did you?' continued Joyce. 'That's why you murdered Lola Parker.'

'What?' The Russian sprang into life. 'No, I didn't! I didn't kill her!' He shook his head. 'I'm sorry for everything. I made a big mistake.' He turned to Miss Kingsley. 'I am particularly sorry to you, Vivien. I was foolish. She never meant anything to me.'

Miss Kingsley dismissed his words with a wave of her hand. She had the expression of a woman who had heard this sort of thing before.

'You were very worried about losing your relationship with Miss Kingsley, weren't you, Mr Volkov?' said Joyce. 'Your relationship with Miss Kingsley gave you status and admiration from others. It was everything you craved, wasn't it? And yet you made the mistake of having an affair with a young woman and Miss Kingsley grew suspicious. You guessed you had one final chance with her. And so the simple solution for you was to murder Lola and hope your secret died with her.'

'No!' said Nikolai. 'I didn't murder Lola! She was a nice girl.' He stopped and checked himself, clearly wondering what Miss Kingsley would make of his words. 'I would never have harmed her. I don't know who did harm her, but it wasn't me.'

'For what it's worth, Detective,' said Miss Kingsley. 'I believe him. I couldn't care less about him now and I want nothing more to do with him. But I'm not ready to admit that he murdered Lola. Despite everything he's done, I don't believe he would have done that.'

'So what about Cedric Langley?' Joyce asked Nikolai. 'Why did you murder him?'

'I didn't,' said Nikolai. 'I didn't murder either of them!'

'He's telling the truth!' said Miss Kingsley.

'I believe him,' said Augusta.

Joyce turned to her. 'You believe Mr Volkov, Augusta? Even though this man clearly wished to silence Lola Parker?'

'But did he wish to silence her?' said Augusta. 'I realise he didn't want news of their affair to spread because then his relationship with Miss Kingsley would come to an end. But he probably sensed the relationship was going to end anyway. I don't think he was desperate enough to murder Lola over it.'

Joyce scratched his head. 'So who did murder Lola Parker and Cedric Langley?'

Chapter 52

'THE PERSON we all suspected at the beginning,' said Augusta. 'Daphne Chatsworth.'

Miss Kingsley gasped. 'Not Daphne!'

'You're going to have to explain this, Augusta,' said Philip.

'Daphne is the obvious suspect because she had the best opportunity,' said Augusta. 'She left the stage early during the final part of the show. Her excuse was her shoes were hurting her, and she needed to take them off. However, she knew Lola Parker was alone in the changing rooms. Once she was there, she found Lola. And then she confronted her.'

'About what?' asked Philip.

'An unusual necklace caught my eye when I was looking around Lola Parker's room.'

'Daphne confronted Lola about a necklace?'

'No. Hear me out. The pendant of the necklace was an enamel egg decorated with jewels. It reminded me of a Fabergé egg.'

Miss Kingsley laughed. 'I don't think Lola would have owned any Fabergé jewellery.'

'No, she probably didn't,' said Augusta. 'The pendant looked like a Fabergé egg, but it could have been an imitation.'

'Fabergé is a Russian jeweller,' said Philip. 'Did you give Lola the necklace, Mr Volkov?'

'Yes, I did,' he said. 'It wasn't Fabergé. But it looked like it.'

'After spotting the necklace, I noticed Daphne Chatsworth wearing an identical pendant,' said Augusta. 'Did you give Miss Chatsworth the same style of necklace?'

The Russian said nothing.

'Oh, out with it, Nikolai. Before I throw another cushion at you!' said Miss Kingsley.

'Yes, I gave Daphne a necklace, too.'

'Does this mean you also had an affair with Miss Chatsworth?' asked Philip.

'Yes.'

'Oh, good grief.' Miss Kingsley got to her feet. 'Don't tell me all my models are wearing fake Fabergé necklaces!'

'No,' said Nikolai. 'Only those two.'

'Oh, only those two. That's alright then.' She went and stood by the window. Augusta noticed her wipe her eyes.

'So Daphne Chatsworth murdered Lola Parker over Nikolai Volkov?' said Philip. 'She was jealous?'

'I think so,' said Augusta. She turned to Nikolai. 'Did you end your affair with Miss Chatsworth to begin an affair with Miss Parker?'

He gave Miss Kingsley an anxious glance before responding. 'Yes.'

'So Miss Chatsworth killed Miss Parker in a jealous rage,' said Joyce.

'Yes,' said Augusta. 'When Lola remained alone in the

changing rooms, Miss Chatsworth must have realised she had an opportunity to confront her about Mr Volkov. She left the stage and returned to the changing rooms. The confrontation must have become physical, and Miss Chatsworth managed to strangle Miss Parker with the scarf which was already tied around her neck. Once Miss Parker was dead, Miss Chatsworth ran out of the changing rooms claiming she'd found her there.'

'And everyone believed her,' said Miss Kingsley, turning away from the window. 'I know I did.'

'You claimed you didn't see Miss Parker when you were alone with her in the changing rooms,' said Philip. 'Was that true?'

'No, I lied. I saw her there, and I shouted at her for refusing to go onto the stage. I told her she was a silly girl, and I wished I'd never hired her.' Her voice cracked with emotion. 'I didn't want to admit it because I felt guilty about it afterwards. And also it gave me a motive to murder her. She was a silly girl, but I could never have harmed her. I'm still struggling to believe Daphne could have done such a thing.'

'It's obvious Miss Chatsworth murdered Cedric Langley too,' said Augusta. 'She visited him at his flat shortly before he died.'

'But why did she do it?' asked Joyce.

'We'll have to ask her.'

Chapter 53

'No one had ever given me attention like that before,' said Daphne Chatsworth.

The sun was setting as they listened to her in the sitting room of her Richmond home. The scent of lilies filled the air.

Daphne wore a knee-length candy pink dress with a large silk bow at the V-shaped neckline. Her hands rested in her lap and a pair of handcuffs bound her wrists together. 'I knew it was wrong,' she continued, 'and I knew Miss Kingsley would be upset about it. But I couldn't help myself. Nikolai was handsome, and he said such nice things to me. And he bought me beautiful gifts. How could I refuse him? It was difficult for us to go to many places because we had to be careful not to be seen together.

'I hoped Nikolai would decide to leave Miss Kingsley, but I realise now he didn't care for me as much as he said he did. And when things happened with Lola, that was it. He didn't want to see me anymore. I saw them in the restaurant together. The restaurant he and I went to some-times. They even sat at the same table in the corner so as not to be noticed. Just like we had! I couldn't believe it. He didn't even have the decency to end things with me properly. He just switched from me to Lola.

'I confronted them both that night in the restaurant. Lola was surprised. She didn't know Nikolai and I had been together. But she thought it was funny. She actually laughed at me. Why would someone be as nasty as that? I wanted to tell Miss Kingsley about them. But if I did that, then Lola would tell her about me and Nikolai. I couldn't win. I hated her.' She turned to Augusta. 'Have you ever hated someone so much you wished they were dead?'

'Oh Daphne, don't say such things?' cried her mother. She had been sobbing ever since Daphne had admitted to Lola Parker's murder.

'I just wanted Lola to suffer,' said Daphne. 'I wanted her to feel the same pain I had felt. She had that scarf on, so I just pulled it. And I pulled it tighter and tighter, and she tried to stop me, but I was stronger. For the first time in my life, I felt powerful. I won.'

Her mother broke out into fresh sobs.

'When Lola fell onto the floor, I realised I had to get myself out of it,' said Daphne. 'So I pretended I'd found her there. And for a while, everyone believed me.'

'You were an obvious suspect from the start, Miss Chatsworth,' said Philip. 'But you're right. People did believe you. You were almost too obvious to be the suspect.'

'And Mr Langley?' said Detective Sergeant Joyce. 'What happened with him?'

'I didn't go to his apartment intending to kill him. I told you the truth when I said I wanted to look at some photographs. But he knew about me and Nikolai. He'd seen us together once in Soho. After that, he used to ask me about Nikolai when there was no one else around. He teased me about it. He thought it was funny. He made jokes about Miss Kingsley being cheated on. He made jokes about Nikolai dropping me for someone else. I couldn't bear his taunting. It was infuriating. I remember he took a photograph of me once and said, "smile and think about Nikolai." When I went to his apartment that day to look at the photographs, all was well. I was just about to leave when he said, "let's frame one of these and send it to Nikolai." He thought it was funny and he had no idea how much his words hurt! I was on my way out when I saw his scarves hanging on the pegs by the door. I decided to teach him a lesson.'

'So you lost your temper with Cedric Langley, just as you had with Lola Parker,' said Augusta.

Daphne nodded. 'I wish now I had just left. But I was filled with rage. I was furious. When I took the scarf, I knew it wouldn't take much to overpower Cedric. Not if he wasn't expecting it. So I went back to his living room. He was sitting in his chair having a cigarette. He didn't see me enter the room, he wasn't expecting me. If he'd seen me, I'm sure he'd have been able to fight me off. But I saw my opportunity to shut him up once and for all. Now he can't laugh at me anymore.'

'You did a good job of convincing everyone you left Cedric Langley before he was murdered,' said Philip. 'You told us you were at his flat for twenty minutes, is that true?'

'Yes, it's true. I attacked him, then I left.'

'And then you met your mother for a shopping trip?'

Daphne nodded. Augusta found it extraordinary she could have carried on with her plans as normal after committing such an atrocity.

Philip turned to Isabella Chatsworth. 'How was your daughter when you met her at three o'clock that day?'

Mrs Chatsworth gave a sniff. 'Very quiet. I knew something was wrong.'

'And you didn't want to tell us that?'

'Of course not! I'd do anything to protect my daughter!'

'Miss Chatsworth did a good job of throwing everyone off the scent when she sent herself a scarf with a threatening note,' said Augusta. 'And for good measure, she sent one to Miss Kingsley, too. She hoped that by doing so, everyone would look elsewhere for the suspect.'

'It was a clever move,' said Joyce. 'And it almost had us all fooled.'

'But not quite,' said Philip. 'It didn't fool Augusta.'

'That's because Miss Chatsworth made quite a show of coming to my shop to show me the scarf and the note,' said Augusta. 'She was a little too keen to show it to me.'

'She tried a little too hard?'

'Yes. That was the mistake she made.'

Chapter 54

'SO MY WORST FEARS ARE CONFIRMED,' said Lady Hereford. Augusta sat with her in her suite at the Russell Hotel. 'There was I trying to defend my great-niece, and she was a murderer all along! You must think me very foolish, Augusta.'

'No, I don't think that at all, Lady Hereford. Daphne is a member of your family. No one wants to think a member of their family is capable of something like this.'

'Yes, I suppose that's what made me blind to her,' said Lady Hereford. 'But when you look at it, my niece, Isabella, is very odd indeed. Perhaps it's not her fault. Perhaps it's my sister's fault. We always called Agnes the black sheep of the family. And maybe that was because of my father. He was odd as well. I loved him very much, of course. But there was word of insanity in his family. Sadly, I wonder if Daphne has inherited that.' She paused and stared out of the window over Russell Square. 'There's probably no use trying to understand why Daphne did this,' she said. 'When things like this happen, we want a proper explanation, don't we, Augusta? And I think sometimes there isn't a proper explanation for why people do these things. And that can be difficult to accept.'

Augusta nodded. 'Daphne was driven by envy and shame. They're natural emotions, but most people are able to live with them. Now and again, you come across a person who can't cope with their emotions. They can only manage by harming other people. I don't know what the reasons for that can be. They're probably many and varied. One thing I have learned is you can never quite predict who might act like that. Whether it's a stranger, a friend, or even a member of your own family. You can never be completely sure.'

Chapter 55

'HARRIET BOUGHT *THE MAYOR OF CASTERBRIDGE*,' said Fred when Augusta returned to her shop.

'Excellent! Did you give her a discount?'

'Yes. I reduced it to two shillings for her.'

'Well done, Fred.'

'And I also…' He trailed off.

'Also what?'

'Asked her if she would like to go to the theatre with me.'

'Oh! And what did she say?'

'She said yes. So we're going to see *The Gipsy Princess* at the Prince of Wales Theatre this weekend.'

'I'm sure you'll have a lovely time.'

Philip descended the stairs. 'I've just got off the telephone to Detective Inspector Morris,' he said. 'He interviewed Lord and Lady Whittington and established that Mr Briggs was the man who'd loaned them *Sunset at the Temple of Artemis*. The painting has been seized and returned to Lord Montpelier. Lord and Lady Whittington feel thoroughly embarrassed by the entire affair. They had no idea the painting was stolen. Briggs and several of his men have been arrested. Briggs isn't talking yet, but some of his men are, and Morris has located some more of the stolen artworks. So it was nice we could help him in the end, wasn't it?'

Augusta nodded. 'It's excellent news. And your family is out of danger now.'

'They are. I'm going to take a trip to Bognor Regis this weekend and see them.'

She tried not to think of him spending time with his wife. 'That's a good idea, Philip. I'm sure they'll be pleased to see you.'

'Perhaps.' He smiled. 'I hope so, anyway. And there's more good news. Eddie Miller has been arrested for pestering a young lady at his workplace, Lyon's factory at Greenford.'

'Good,' said Augusta. 'He seems to make a habit of doing that. I hope he's locked up for it.'

'Me too. Have you got any plans for this weekend, Augusta?'

'No. But I shall keep Lady Hereford company. She's still very upset about Daphne.'

'I'm not surprised. Well, if you'd been at a loose end, I would have suggested you come with me down to Bognor. You've never met my wife, Audrey, have you?'

'No. That would be…'

'Nice?'

'Of course. I hope you have a good time, Philip.'

The End

Historical Note

In the early twentieth century, fashion models were called mannequins and were often friends and clients of the designer or in-house seamstresses. I chose not to use the word mannequin to describe the models in this book because I associate it too much with the plastic mannequins in clothing stores! With the rise of haute couture in 1920s Paris, the model profession gained importance. Commercial publishing grew quickly at this time and the latest fashions were modelled by society girls and actresses in publications such as *Vogue*. Women such as Hannah Lee Sherman and Marion Morehouse were early 'supermodels', paving the way for many women to pursue modelling as a career. Fashion photography flourished at this time, pioneered by photographers such as Edward Steichen and Adolphe de Meyer.

There were several successful lady fashion designers in the early twentieth century: Lanvin, Elsa Schiaparelli, Sonia Delaunay, Hilda Steward and Gabrielle (Coco) Chanel. The character of Vivien Kingsley was inspired by them and their lives (I'm assuming they were more likeable!). Chanel was establishing herself as a couturiere in Paris in the early 1920s. Her brief affair with the exiled Grand Duke Dmitri Pavlovich of Russia around this time is an inspiration for the storyline between Vivien Kingsley and Nikolai Volkov.

Holland Park Rink in west London was opened by the American Rink Co in December 1909. According to an edition Sporting Life from 24 December 1909, the rink was the 'largest in the world erected for roller skating'. It had over 75,000 feet of floor space and the skating area was made of the 'finest Michigan maple'. It was a fashionable venue in Edwardian times, with aristocratic roller skaters being pictured on the pages of *Tatler* magazine. The rink was also used for other sporting events and shows - including fashion shows. After WWI, the rink appears to have been mainly used for dog shows and boxing matches. The venue declined in popularity during the 1920s and closed in 1928. It was used as a garage for a while before being demolished to make way for a hotel in 1973 - today it's the Hilton London Kensington.

Kensington's large, elegant townhouses have long made it a desirable area for the wealthy. Kensington Palace was the birthplace and childhood home of Queen Victoria and continues to be a residence for members of the royal family. Kensington is also renowned for its museums, including the Victoria and Albert Museum, the Natural History Museum, and the Science Museum.

Holland House was built in 1605 by the diplomat and politician, Sir Walter Cope. At that time, its Kensington location was rural and the entire estate was five hundred acres in size. King James I and King William III were visitors. Over the centuries, much of the land was sold off for development. London's rapid growth during this time must have made the land very valuable.

During the nineteenth century, famous visitors to the house included Lord Byron, Charles Dickens, Benjamin Disraeli and Sir Walter Scott. The last major event at the house was a debutante ball held in 1939 for Rosalind Cubitt, the mother of Queen Camilla. The ball was attended by George VI and Queen Elizabeth. The following year, the house was destroyed by incendiary bombs during the Blitz in WWII.

The ruined building was preserved and sold to the London County Council in 1952. The remaining land became Holland Park, which is now a popular public space with a cafe, restaurant, play areas and an open-air theatre. The park lends its name to the Holland Park area of Kensington.

Spitalfields, in east London, became a haven for French Huguenots fleeing religious persecution in the seventeenth century. The refugees brought silk weaving skills with them and transformed the area into a hub of the silk industry. The Spitalfields silk weavers were renowned for their intricate designs and high-quality fabrics, which became highly sought after in London's fashion scene. In the nineteenth century, the industry faced challenges, such as competition from imported silks and industrialisation. By the late nineteenth century, buildings had fallen into disrepair and the area was blighted by poverty. Many of the weavers' houses were demolished as the area was redeveloped during the twentieth century. In recent years, the area has gentrified and many of the remaining weavers' houses have been beautifully restored. There are conservation efforts underway to preserve the rest.

Sunset at the Temple of Artemis is a fictional painting. And the painter R C Riverhouse is fictional too.

The Temple of Artemis - or the Temple of Diana - was one of the Seven Wonders of the Ancient World. Located in the ancient city of Ephesus (in present-day Turkey), it was dedicated to the goddess Artemis. The temple was renowned for its grandeur and architectural beauty and underwent several reconstructions because of destruction by natural disasters and arson. An expedition sponsored by the British Museum rediscovered the site of the temple in 1869. Fragments of the temple are today displayed at the museum and a few fragments remain at the original site.

The Dockland Murder

An Augusta Peel Mystery Book 9

In the bustling heart of London's docklands, a prominent shipping magnate is found dead. When Scotland Yard calls on Augusta Peel, she realises she has a puzzling connection to the case.

As she delves deeper into the labyrinthine alleys and shadowy warehouses of the docks, Augusta must use her skills and courage to untangle the mystery before the killer strikes again.

Find out more here: mybook.to/dockland-murder

Thank you

Thank you for reading this Augusta Peel mystery, I really hope you enjoyed it!

Would you like to know when I release new books? Here are some ways to stay updated:

- Like my Facebook page: facebook.com/emilyorganwriter
- Follow me on Goodreads: goodreads.com/emily_organ
- Follow me on BookBub: bookbub.com/authors/emily-organ
- View my other books here: emilyorgan.com

And if you have a moment, I would be very grateful if you would leave a quick review online. Honest reviews of my books help other readers discover them too!

Also by Emily Organ

Penny Green Series:

Limelight
The Rookery
The Maid's Secret
The Inventor
Curse of the Poppy
The Bermondsey Poisoner
An Unwelcome Guest
Death at the Workhouse
The Gang of St Bride's
Murder in Ratcliffe
The Egyptian Mystery
The Camden Spiritualist

Churchill & Pemberley Series:

Tragedy at Piddleton Hotel
Murder in Cold Mud
Puzzle in Poppleford Wood

Also by Emily Organ

Trouble in the Churchyard
Wheels of Peril
The Poisoned Peer
Fiasco at the Jam Factory
Disaster at the Christmas Dinner
Christmas Calamity at the Vicarage (novella)

Writing as Martha Bond

Lottie Sprigg Travels Mystery Series:

Murder in Venice
Murder in Paris
Murder in Cairo
Murder in Monaco
Murder in Vienna

Lottie Sprigg Country House Mystery Series:

Murder in the Library
Murder in the Grotto
Murder in the Maze
Murder in the Bay

Printed in Great Britain
by Amazon